The Painted Man

A Speculative Fiction Review Book Published by
SpeculativeFictionReview.com

www.speculativefictionreview.com

ISBN: 0-9785232-1-0

Cover art by Peter Dingus.

The Painted Man

www.speculativefictionreview.com

Dedication

To my cousin Krystal, hoping her health improves and her spirits soar. And to my son Parker, whom I hope to inspire to follow his own dreams as he grows up.

Chapter One

April 4, 2003, 2:13am, 55 Miles north of Baghdad, Iraq.

Bursts of light and sound punctuated the night sky over Iraq as anti-aircraft rounds popped and crackled in response to falling bombs. The gunners continued their air saturation strategy, hoping for that one lucky shot, a golden BB, to bring down a phantom enemy. The incoming firepower concentrated on a large Presidential Palace complex near Lake Tharthar. Occasionally, a bomb found a high-priority target amongst the maze of structures. One particular building on the eastern outskirts of the complex drew more attention than most.

The crumbling walls of the massive stone structure surrounded the completely destroyed interior. Still, the bombs rained down on the rubble because the building itself was not the main target. The aboveground shell acted merely as a façade, shielding a subsurface structure.

Deep within the heavily fortified concrete bunker, a swarm of activity persisted throughout the intense bombing. The soldiers inside knew they were protected against most ordnance and merely paused each time their fortress shook.

A huge sunken room at the hub of the bunker served as the command center. General Shakir Amin al Duri commanded a small contingent of loyal soldiers and civilian staff from a communications console at the center of the floor. From there, he could see everything important to his operation, including the bunker entrance above him. A rickety metal staircase led to a massive steel door complete with electromagnetic locking pins. For now,

General Duri seemed more interested in a glass-enclosed room beyond the edge of the sunken command center. He watched impatiently while bellowing orders in Arabic.

A tall, imposing figure, the general commanded respect with each word and every glance. His subjects nervously jumped into action at his every demand. As he grew more impatient, Duri meticulously preened himself, grooming a thick mustache by constantly straightening tufts of the course hair.

The blinds inside the glass room finally opened and Duri glided over to survey the progress of the most important aspect of this operation. Through the window, he observed a bewildered soldier, Mahmud Jafari, dressed only in his skivvies and seated on the surgical table in the center of the room. He rubbed sore skin while doctors monitored his blood pressure and changed out an IV bag. Duri continued tugging at his mustache, but with far less tenacity.

Lieutenant Ibrahim Salih Khalifa al Hashimi, an officer under Duri's command, said a few words to the patient and turned to exit. Duri fixated on the dazed soldier inside, even as Hashimi approached. The lieutenant waited a few moments, then hesitantly interrupted Duri's thoughts. "General."

Without turning, Duri spoke in a much softer tone than before. "Is he ready?"

Hashimi nervously fiddled with his hands. "I have given him his instructions, but he still needs a little time to recover from his sleep."

Duri, visibly disturbed by the remark, turned and faced Hashimi. "No, he must go now. The Americans are here."

"But I have only given him his first contact. That is all he knows."

The general turned his attention back to the room. "That is exactly all he needs to know! Prepare the exit, quickly, before the door is breached!"

The officers working nearby tried to act as if they had not heard the scolding. But Hashimi knew better. He ducked his head shamefully and backed away. "Yes General." Dutifully, he went about his task, leaving Duri to tend to the confused soldier.

Duri stepped inside the room where the doctors scurried about, putting away equipment. Another man in the opposite corner quietly cleaned his own instruments. All of them remained oblivious to the presence of a superior officer. But the bleary-eyed patient watched intently as the general closed the blinds and the door.

Then Duri raised his Glock 22 sidearm and aimed at the unsuspecting doctor to his right. With military precision, he fired, killing the man with a silenced .40 caliber round to the right temple. Duri swung the pistol slightly to the left without hesitation and fired two more rounds into the back of the next victim. The jolting body slumped awkwardly forward, catching the eye of the third doctor, now standing behind the operating table at the center of the room. The stunned patient froze at the sight of his superior officer aiming a gun in his direction.

The general, moving in a continuous arc, fired one shot over the stunned soldier's left shoulder, putting a bullet in the third doctor's forehead. Duri passed the left side of the table, never breaking stride or lowering the weapon.

The fourth and final target now scrambled in fear along the back wall, but had no chance to escape. General Duri's final prey fell forward into a surgical prep tray as a round tore into his left shoulder blade. The instruments slashed his face and arms while he reached desperately for something to break his fall. As the fourth victim crashed to the ground, Duri moved in and finished him off with another slug to the head.

A final bullet punctured the skull of the second victim, and Duri retired his weapon to its holster. He spared the shocked patient, who had barely moved during the entire ordeal.

Duri acted as if this were business as usual, and approached the soldier, who regarded him wide-eyed. "Mahmud, I am General Duri. You are about to embark on a very important mission for your country. I have chosen you for this operation because you have a very special quality. You have nothing left to lose. No family, and no hope for a career. I know you will succeed."

Duri encircled the disorientated man, handing him a fully-loaded 9mm handgun. Mahmud accepted, and closely eyed the murderer now reaching in from behind. Duri finished tying a blindfold around Mahmud's head, then walked briskly toward the door.

"Soldier, do you know the details of your first contact?" Duri asked.

As he reached the door, Mahmud set the gun on the table. He sensed the lights go out and carefully stood.

"Yes, General. But I know nothing else of my mission." His head followed the direction of footsteps trailing to his right. The silence did nothing to allay his fears. An overwhelming force filled the room, as if the souls of the four dead men had surrounded Mahmud in the darkness. Then, a clicking sound brought the faintest light.

Duri walked through the eerie greenish glow to the silhouette in the center of the room. "Take two steps forward."

Mahmud complied nervously. As he entered the aura of light, an intricate, fluorescent yellow tattoo composed mostly of Arabic writing emerged, covering ninety percent of his exposed skin. Another click brought darkness again. "Take off the blindfold and get dressed. You will be leaving soon."

The soldier faithfully followed orders as the bright overhead lights shot on. Duri approached the young man and spoke, this time like a father. "I am truly sorry about your family. Their deaths were indeed tragic. Your father and your brothers were all fine soldiers."

Mahmud suddenly felt ill, seeing something dubious in this killer's eyes. After the general exited the room, Mahmud scanned the bodies, all of them bleeding from well-placed bullet holes to the forehead. The scene reminded him of a recent day when he walked into his parents' home and found six dead family members. Quickly, fear overcame his rage and nearly paralyzed his body. Then Duri popped his head in the doorway.

"We must go!"

Moments later, they reached the hidden exit in the hallway. A few soldiers cleared away dilapidated machinery, while others rushed fully-armed toward the command room. Pounding noises from that direction could only mean the Americans had found the door. Duri reached up to the earthen wall and unhooked the corner of an ornate rug, revealing a dark tunnel entrance behind.

Hashimi handed Mahmud a high-beam flashlight and nudged him toward the opening. He took the cue and brushed hastily past Duri, his shadow quickly disappearing into the tunnel. Hashimi waited a few moments, then started toward the cave. But the general interceded, holding a gun to his lieutenant's head. "Change of plans. You stay here."

"But the Americans…" An explosion followed by bursts of gunfire interrupted his plea. Duri nodded at the two soldiers and backed into the tunnel. As they concealed the exit, Hashimi grew enraged at this cowardly betrayal.

Chapter Two

Colonel Warren Block, commander of an Army Intelligence unit in Baghdad, lumbered down the rickety metal staircase to the bunker's sunken command center. He dwarfed the men behind him, as well as most of the Army Rangers now occupying the complex. His size, combined with a brutal scowl and scarred face, forced everyone to notice. Seasoned soldiers hastily cleared the way as he reached the floor.

Block's attention immediately locked on the surgical room to his right. Inside, Colonel Tim Holt directed the activity surrounding dead bodies and smashed equipment. They were treating this as a crime scene investigation, with Block taking over as lead detective. The colonels exchanged salutes, then handshakes.

Block tried to make sense of the scene, then gave up. "What is all this equipment?" He glanced at the soldiers standing around. "I'm pretty sure your boys didn't assassinate these unarmed men."

"Damn right they didn't. We're not a bunch of jarheads straight out of boot camp. Someone did this before we got here. The equipment was blown with a couple of grenades before we even secured the entrance. Made enough of a mess to keep us guessing about the equipment for awhile."

Block tensed. "Well, I'm mainly interested in the survivors. One of them should know what this is all about. But considering four were murdered, I'm not too hopeful they'll talk."

"We've questioned them already. We'll transfer custody of the tapes to you immediately. Come with me, there's one guy you'll be very interested in." They turned to leave the room. "His name is Lieutenant Ibrahim Salih Khalifa al Hashimi. He's a character. Already asked for a nice house in Connecticut in exchange for information."

Block cracked his knuckles on the way to the holding area. He resembled a prize fighter preparing for his next bout. "And you found him here?"

Holt nodded. "Yeah, why?"

"No reason."

Past the concealed tunnel entrance, Block and Holt found a heavy metal door flanked by Rangers. They entered and tested the shackles securing their informant to a pipe against the back wall. Holt surveyed the pathetic scene, then turned to the guards. "Take off his handcuffs. Leave his legs shackled."

After one of the soldiers uncuffed the man, both guards left the room. Holt pulled out a box of cigarettes and presented one to his prisoner. "This is Colonel Warren Block with Army Intelligence. Sorry about the smokes. Best I can do on short notice."

Hashimi, rubbing his sore wrists, studied the enormous man standing stone-faced by the door. Block's presence made him even more nervous than usual. He anxiously fumbled with the cigarette as Holt lit it.

"I'll give you a little warning, Hashimi. You'll be in his custody soon," he gestured toward Block. "I won't be able to protect you anymore. The boys down at Army Intelligence do some freaky shit to uncooperative prisoners. Your best bet is to give us something we can work with before we transfer you over. You understand everything I'm saying so far?"

"Yes, yes. My English is good. Just talk slow."
Hashimi inhaled mightily, keeping a constant eye on
Block. "I want a lawyer. Make sure I get my house in
America."

Block sprung forward and thrust his huge hand into
Hashimi's throat, slamming the small man's head against
the pipe. "Listen, I don't know what your game is, but as
far as I'm concerned, you're either a terrorist or a prisoner
of war. Either way, you're not getting a lawyer."

Hashimi cringed and lamented the broken cigarette
lying on the floor. "I have heard this American phrase—
'you catch more flies with honey.' You prefer a
flyswatter, right?" A sly smile forced Block away and
Holt traded places with the angry giant.

Another lit cigarette made the prisoner happy again.
Holt let Hashimi have an extended drag, then patted him
on the shoulders. "I can guarantee you asylum in the U.S.,
but not a house."

Block groaned. "Holt, you don't understand. This man
can't be trusted."

"What makes you so sure?"

Block had nothing specific to offer and silently
stepped away. Hashimi merrily puffed away. "See, this is
much better. I help you now."

Minutes later, he led the soldiers to the pile of
machinery. With free hands and legs, he waved proudly at
the junk pile. "Remove the machines and I show you
something interesting."

The two guards lowered their weapons and heaved the
metal out of the way. Hashimi then ripped the rug from
the wall with dramatic effect. The two colonels stepped
forward with renewed interest.

Holt asked, "Why didn't you escape?"

"I try. The General stopped me."

"What general?"

"General Duri. The man from the surgery left, and I was to follow. Then the General goes instead."

Holt called out to his unit and a dozen men rushed over. He directed them to enter the cave while Block escorted his informant to the surgical room.

Inside, Block pointed at the bodies. "Did the general kill these men?"

Hashimi appeared horrified. "He must have killed them. I did not see."

"What about the surgery? What kind of surgery did they perform?"

"I do not know. I only planned his first contact. The General knows everything, but I only know where he goes first. But now, the General goes and not me. Maybe the plan has changed."

Block moved in close, nose to forehead. "Then tell me where you were supposed to go first."

Hashimi stepped back. Before he could answer, a nearby explosion rocked the room. Block led Hashimi by the arm to the source of the blast. The tunnel bellowed dust into the hallway, causing widespread coughing. Block found Holt amidst the chaos and helped him to his feet. "Are you OK?"

"I'm fine. Don't worry, it was just a robot. No one has actually gone in yet."

Block sighed, then pulled his sidearm. Hashimi's eyes lit up as Block whipped around and shoved the gun's barrel into his mouth. "Did you know about this?"

Hashimi tried to speak, but could only shake his head.

Holt stepped in. "Colonel, nobody got hurt."

"Yeah, you're right, but I'm taking him back to Command as a ghost. No paperwork. He doesn't exist for now." He holstered his weapon, then exchanged salutes with Holt before leaving his friend to clean up the mess.

* * *

Mahmud Jafari climbed a built-in ladder until he bumped his head against a metal access hatch. Though covered with sand, it opened easily. After cleaning the grains from his eyes, Mahmud climbed out onto the down slope of a small earthen berm. The daylight blinded him temporarily before revealing his new surroundings. Ahead, a marketplace at the edge of a fairly large city bustled with activity.

Because of the complex underground maze he had just traversed, Mahmud had no idea where he was. The buildings did not look familiar. After covering the hatch, he approached the nearest buildings from the rear while surveying the crowd. Far to his left, an American military checkpoint controlled vehicular access to the area. He noticed that the occupiers appeared to be sticking to the perimeter of the city.

The celebratory crowd ignored his presence, buying food and defacing posters of Saddam Hussein. Walking amongst his countrymen, Mahmud nervously checked his watch and rubbed his sore skin. Deeper within the city limits, he found a small, partially destroyed statue. After a final time check, he unfurled a yellow scarf and displayed it prominently around his forehead.

No one noticed as he paraded down the center of the road, back and forth. Then, a small rust bucket of a truck pulled away from a distant alley and soon found Mahmud. Upon exchanging passwords, the driver took his new passenger in the direction of the checkpoint. Pedestrians slowly parted, letting them pass toward their next destination, and their next contact.

* * *

General Duri watched the first rendezvous from a fruit stand at the edge of town. Hiding behind the other patrons, he waited for the car to pass. Then he placed his own yellow scarf on his head and stepped past the crowd. Seconds later, he too was picked up.

The driver paused and handed Duri a playing card. He smirked at the image. "At least I'm not the Ace of Spades."

The driver chuckled and drove off the road toward the ridge. Duri gave him a sideways glance.

"Don't worry. I've never been stuck in the sand in this car."

Duri tugged a little at his mustache and tightened his grip on the door. "Just get me past the checkpoints and I'll take over the wheel."

Chapter Three

American soldiers guarded a section of the opulent Radwaniyah Presidential Palace complex at the western edge of Baghdad. To the south, coalition forces fought to secure the rest of the 9.3 square mile complex and cleared pockets of resistance still defending Saddam International Airport. Sporadic gunfire and frequent explosions could be heard a short distance from the coalition's newest acquisition.

Inside the complex, the Army worked to set up a fully-operational military base, including a center for intelligence operations commanded by Colonel Block. The main palace building, situated along the banks of the Tigris River, suited his needs, given its proximity to the sector's main entrance and the stockade. It stood amongst many lavish buildings once used by the former dictator, and now borrowed by the coalition.

The soldiers assigned to the intelligence unit had made great progress converting the palace into a functional military center. Block and his superiors had laid out explicit instructions for the center's design.

The lower level housed main operations, with its grand foyer and open, spacious rooms. Block had the enormous banquet room just off the main foyer converted to an interrogation center, complete with an observation room in the adjoining butler's pantry. A large two-way mirror conveniently separated the 600 square foot pantry from the interrogation room. Behind the opaque glass, state-of-the-art monitoring equipment replaced the wine and dishes. From there, the experts could utilize their equipment to detect lies and immediately communicate with the interrogators on the other side of the glass.

A set of double doors led past the observation room to the main kitchen. Block grabbed a cup of coffee from the counter and stepped into what used to be a formal reception room. Now it held the computer and communications nerve center he needed to stay connected to the command center just a few buildings away.

Along with Lieutenant Doug Sedal, a technical genius and his right-hand man, Block reviewed the communications log for the past week. They were looking for anything referencing a major operation launched from the Lake Tharthar palace bunker. As they worked over the logs, Block was distracted by the sharp echoes of a woman's shoes on the hard marble floor. He glanced up and was surprised at the sight of a beautiful woman staring down at him.

She was out of uniform and seemingly out of place in a war zone. He couldn't help admiring her petite, slightly muscular physique, and the black flowing hair that accentuated her exotic beauty. With smooth dark skin, she could pass for an Arab, but her clothing was that of a Westerner.

She adeptly recognized Block as the senior officer and approached him. Extending her hand revealed the 9mm on her hip. "Colonel Block? I'm Special Agent Shana Reid with the CIA."

Block delicately shook her hand, but his smile drooped. "You just ruined a nice fantasy I had going. You want to be careful walking around here armed; you might get yourself shot by one of these idiots."

"Well, thanks for looking out for little ol' me, but being dark helped me get this assignment. And the fact that I'm an expert on Arabic studies didn't hurt."

"That's good to know," Block said, more than a little put off. "I'll try and remember that. Now what assignment are you talking about? I'm not expecting any CIA."

"Oh, yeah, I forgot to mention that," said Sedal meekly.

Block paused, then hardened. "Mention what, Lieutenant?"

"Agent Reid here and another CIA operative were sent to assist with the Tharthar case."

Block seethed. "Sent by who?"

"The President, sir. Special orders. He wants the CIA to coordinate with the military from this camp. They're planning to conduct the WMD searches from here. Agent Reid was already on her way to help set up the team when the Oval Office caught wind of the hidden tunnels and missing soldier."

Block glared impatiently at him. "That would have been nice to know."

Reid regarded Block, amused, and folded her arms as if to say, I guess you won't be getting rid of me any time soon.

"Well, I suppose it could be worse. At least this time I got someone easy on the eyes and not some obnoxious hillbilly like that last agent in Afghanistan. Remember that guy, Sedal?" The lieutenant nodded knowingly and continued reviewing his field reports.

Reid smiled. "You're not going to like my partner very much, then. He's outside unloading equipment. Should be here any moment."

As she finished the statement, the longest, tallest Texan that Block had ever seen strode through the adjacent tea parlor, now a computer server farm, and headed in Reid's direction. Agent Lonnie "Buzz" Foster looked the part of a West Texas saddle hand, from his bent and dirty palm leaf cowboy hat down to his dusty boots. Block glared at Reid with a sick look. "I don't have the time or patience to deal with this shit, lady."

Reid met Buzz just inside the doorway and helped him unload three packed duffel bags. "Thanks for bringing those in. You're a true gentleman."

"My pleasure, ma'am." The accent brought moans from both men working the computers. Buzz spotted the senior officer and humbly removed his hat. "Howdy, I'm Buzz Foster," he declared, extending his hand.

Block responded in kind, then introduced his lieutenant. Buzz displayed a goofy, toothpicked smile even as Block tried to crush his hand in a male, territorial display. With the pleasantries out of the way, the colonel abruptly turned his back.

"Buzz, Reid, I have a lot of work here, so make yourselves at home. Just don't venture too far south," said Block. Then he caught a glimpse of Buzz. "And for God's sake, put your hat back on. We're not in the old west, and you're not under my command."

Buzz smirked down at Reid and adjusted his hat. "You got it, chief. Well, Colonel, one of the soldiers out front said they couldn't get that camera working at the checkpoint," Buzz said. "I'll let agent Reid work out our arrangements while I go help 'em out with that." With a tip of his hat, Buzz left.

16

Block tossed a folder on the desk and sighed. "What is that jackass talking about?"

"Don't underestimate him. He can fix anything that's broke, destroy anything that isn't, and do it all under your nose without you ever seeing him. His file reads like he's ten agents," said Reid.

Her defiant tone impressed Block. "OK, so what do you need?"

"We need a wired room, networked computer stations, and a place to sleep. And we need to talk about how we are going to cooperate on this mission."

"Cooperate? You mean I'm supposed to baby-sit you guys? No way. The Army has plenty of resources to catch these targets on our own."

Reid pulled a satellite phone from one of the bags and powered it up.

Block scowled. "What are you doing?"

"Calling the President. Your full name is Warren Block, is that right?"

Block was not amused. "Hang it up. I get you. The lieutenant here will set up your quarters and wire the room for you. You'll each get a cot and two blankets. The kitchen has chow, water, and coffee. I'll meet you in the interrogation room for a status report in one hour. No matter what, though, you tell me everything you know when you know it. If not, I'll call the President myself."

"Agreed. But that better be a big room. I look forward to working with you." Reid half smiled, then followed the lieutenant to her new office and quarters in the opposite wing of the palace.

Chapter Four

Buzz snaked his way through the maze of hallways in the palace's north wing. He wondered how one man could justify such a place at the expense of his own people. And there were many more extravagant palaces throughout the country. His own childhood home near Marfa, Texas consisted of only 1,200 square feet and two bedrooms for five people. Buzz envisioned the fate of the former Iraqi leader, hiding and sleeping in shacks, constantly on the run. It gave him a sense of pride and justice.

Continuing through the corridors, Buzz stopped every passing soldier to ask directions to his room. None of them had any idea what he was talking about. Then, two doors down, agent Reid leaned into the hallway to gather her bags. Buzz strode over to help.

Their new office and sleeping space was a big square room with white walls and a small closet. The wood floor, like much of this wing, shined from a high polish. Buzz noted the lack of windows and realized the empty room across the hall had a nice view of the river. "So, is this the best you could do?"

"Block's tough; I think we did pretty well, considering," said Reid.

"Ah, he's a good guy. I probably wouldn't want a couple of yahoos like us interfering either." Buzz started to unpack equipment and set up a makeshift computer console.

"You're an idealistic person. I don't think Block sees the good like you do."

"Doesn't mean we can't work together like civilized folks. He's probably a reasonable guy once you figure out what buttons to push."

"He doesn't like you nearly as much as you like him. And I can already tell he's a chauvinist."

They took a break and leaned on wobbly tables that would be their desks. Buzz unwrapped a half-melted chocolate bar and licked the wrapper. He offered her one.

Reid made a sour face. "That's disgusting."

"You're not some kind of health nut, are you?"

"You think I look like this naturally?"

Buzz looked her up and down, admiring her short, but toned physique. "You're right. Just keep doing whatever you're doing."

Reid blushed. "Remember cowboy, I'm technically your superior on this assignment."

Buzz tipped his hat with a boyish grin. "Yes, ma'am."

"So, let's get to work. We have a line out, but they still need to finish wiring the room. I'm going to bypass the servers for now. I need to contact a list of agents in theater and I don't have time to wait for the Army to hook us up. These agents will be reporting directly to me now, and I need to know what they know quickly."

Buzz grabbed the laptop and plugged it into the outside line. "We don't even have electricity."

"That's what I mean. They have to run a line from the generators. The laptop's juiced up enough for now, though."

"I'll go talk to the lieutenant. He looks like a fellow technophile. I'll get 'em to speed up the process a little."

Reid went to work as he left. She had plenty of data to review and a meeting with Block to attend. The outside

19

line worked, and soon she was on a secure CIA server reading reports from the network of undercover field agents in Iraq. With each report, she posted a message establishing contact protocol and new information regarding her investigation. After a final upload, Reid secured the room and headed for her next encounter with Block.

* * *

Near the center of the southern city of Basrah, agent Mark Naseth lay prone atop an abandoned multi-story building. Through high-powered binoculars, he monitored a storefront across the street with its adjoining second story residence. Like Reid, Naseth passed as an Iraqi, though his considerable skills would be put to better use as an analyst. But the coalition had a shortage of suitable field agents.

Naseth volunteered for the assignment, eager to work in the field. Besides, his knowledge of Arab affairs and the language far exceeded even that of agent Reid. He knew how to act in this environment.

Basrah had been surrounded by British soldiers since the outset of the war, but militants controlled the city, using its citizens as human shields. Naseth had never witnessed this level of conflict, and did his best to stay out of sight, away from the violent edge of town. Conveniently enough for him, the subject he was shadowing had his base of operations in this relatively safe area. He heard gunfire and intermittent explosions in the distance, but not too close to be concerned.

A nervous man puffing wildly on a cigarette emerged from an alley far to the left of Naseth's position. Naseth locked on him immediately, watching through the lenses. Right on time, he thought. The man continued toward his subject's hideout, checking his rear constantly.

Soon he reached the glass door of the storefront and tapped a familiar pattern. Naseth had already witnessed this scene on each of the last four days. How foolish not to vary his routine, he thought.

The subject inside, the main focus of Naseth's investigation, answered the door, scanning the street out front in the usual manner. When he was sure there was nothing out of the ordinary, the nervous man entered. At this point in the daily exchange, Naseth was mainly blind. He needed eyes and ears on the inside. So far, his repeated requests for high-tech assistance had gone unanswered. Considering these men were foreign terrorists, he needed a way inside, sooner rather than later.

For now, Naseth continued training his outdated parabolic mike on the front windows of the store. He only heard the initial exchange of pleasantries, followed by muffled conversation from the back of the building. Minutes later, the man exited through the front door, carrying a lighter load than before. Naseth surmised they had exchanged materials this time as well as information.

As the man shuffled down the street, he seemed to catch a glimpse of Naseth's head poking above the building's façade. He shielded his eyes from the sun's glare and studied the rooftop. After a few minutes without movement, the man slowly turned and walked away. Naseth, now at street level, hunched his shoulders and began to follow.

Chapter Five

The new Baghdad headquarters of the CIA now had all the hook-ups and electricity the two agents could ever need. Buzz used one of the new outlets to test a piece of equipment brought in from the bunker's surgical room. For now, he could not identify the strange contraption, but he realized it had a light fixture as a main component. He examined and pieced together the smashed bulbs, trying to get a handle on its purpose.

"Reid, do we have access to a forensic lab?"

"The best we can do is shuttle evidence over to the mobile units before they're fully-operational. The goal is to assess their readiness as soon as possible so we can get them in the field hunting for WMDs. That won't happen until the rest of the team makes their way to Iraq. So you've got a little time."

"Good, I need them to identify a substance for me before they move out. I need to know what residues are on the inside of these shards of broken glass."

"I don't even think we have the protocol in place for processing evidence."

"It's OK. I need a quick answer on this. I'll retest them later under the official protocol if we need the results for legal reasons. Right now, I just need something to follow."

"Where does the glass come from?"

"This unit I'm trying to rebuild is from the surgical room in the bunker. A little reverse engineering. These ballasts, acting like a transformer, give electricity to the bulbs. It basically reduces the voltage coming from the wall plug. The current put out by the ballasts is more than you'd expect."

"So this isn't your ordinary light source. Maybe it's used in surgery. Some sort of medical device."

"Could be. But the glass pieces have a residue that ordinary fluorescent or neon lights don't. Or at least that's what I want tested. My theory is this unit puts out some different kind of light spectrum. I'm no medical expert, so I can't imagine how that would be used in surgery."

"Well, considering its proximity to the surgical bed, I wouldn't rule it out."

"One thing's for sure. Someone tried to blow the hell out of this thing."

Reid thumped a file in her hand. "Probably our escaped general. Whoever wanted those doctors dead probably tossed the grenades in that room. By the way, one of those men wasn't a doctor; at least he doesn't appear to be."

"How did you find out all this? Did it come from Block?"

"I had to get most of this information from other sources. The colonel has not been very cooperative so far."

Buzz just grunted and turned back to the equipment, bagging pieces of glass and metal, pausing only to finish off another half-melted chocolate bar. Reid chomped on celery while checking more messages posted by field agents.

The one from Mark Naseth interested her immediately. A few more keystrokes lit up a plasma screen hanging on the back wall. Buzz noticed and studied the image of a familiar map. A box outlined the city of Basrah, then zoomed in. A blinking red light near the city's center appeared to be Reid's focus. With a few more clicks, the image closed in tighter.

"I'm going to overlay this on a satellite image and cross reference the location with our files. I'll have to patch into the server in D.C. so it'll take some time to run a check."

"What's Naseth doing in the field? I thought he was an analyst?" asked Buzz.

"I know, but he's come up with some interesting information. The red represents coordinates taken from a laser designator. It's a suspected foreign terrorist hideout that has been getting daily visits from an Iraqi provincial official. The foreigner in the hideout is thought to be al Qaeda, but he's definitely a Pakistani national."

"When did these visits start?"

"Four days ago, according to this schedule. Naseth saw no one there for two weeks prior to that. This official who's been visiting is very close to Saddam's upper echelon. Should be good friends with our missing general. I bet Hashimi could make the connection."

"Looks like we need to get inside that hideout. I'll get a ride in and meet Naseth if you'll get these tested for me."

She shot him an incredulous look. "You're pretty brave, cowboy. A white, six-foot-four man getting inside Basrah right now? The British Army won't even go in."

"Armies act like elephants. I'm going in as a mouse."

She was still not convinced.

"Don't worry. You've seen my file. I've gone into much worse," Buzz said.

Recalling his file, she had to admit he had a point. "OK, let's get you set up. Got anyone back home you want me to say anything to when you don't come back?" Buzz just smiled and started packing.

* * *

Agent Reid found Block in the observation room overlooking the interrogation area. She entered loudly, trying to get his attention. Block nonchalantly glanced in her direction, then turned back to the computer, which only irritated her more.

"Why am I being denied access to the prisoner? You kicked Buzz out of the stockade when he visited earlier, and he was starting to make progress with Hashimi. It's bad enough I had to find out about the escaped general on my own. Now I'm not even allowed to interrogate a key member of his command?"

Without looking up, he responded calmly. "If you want to talk to my prisoner, then follow procedures. You make a formal request and interrogate him here. We'll observe and record everything. Besides, they just brought him in. I have a few questions for him of my own."

"Fine, I'm formally requesting to be included. Now, what about you not sharing information on the escape of one of our most wanted?"

The door to the interrogation room opened and Hashimi, their new favorite informant, walked in under guard. Block noticed and gathered his papers. "You want to know something? Read the reports. You have full access to all our files." This time Block was standing and more perturbed. "Now, if you'll excuse me, I have a witness to question. You can come in, but don't interrupt me or I'll have you thrown out."

Reid reluctantly moved away from the door and followed the uncooperative blockhead into the larger room. Hashimi sat on the other side of the table and glared arrogantly at the two enemy agents as they entered. Block prepared his files and fumbled with an earpiece. A verbal signal from someone in the observation room initiated the interrogation.

"This is agent Shana Reid with the CIA; she's only here to observe," said Block.

Hashimi nodded and grinned. "Thank you. I will observe her with great interest."

Before Block could respond, Reid stood, palms on the table, eyes drilling into Hashimi. "What do you know about foreign terrorists working inside Basrah?"

Block balked, stunned by the question. "What the hell?"

She shot him a fierce look. "Don't expect me to share with you until you start cooperating with me."

The colonel slammed a file on the table and jerked a chair around to sit in. In spite of his anger, he needed to know the answer to that question too.

Chapter Six

General Duri lay prone, peaking over the top of a
sandy knoll protruding from otherwise flat terrain. He
used high-powered binoculars to peer through a thick
cloud of dust and focused on a distant abandoned
farmhouse. This arid land northwest of Lake Tharthar,
without the benefit of irrigation, had long since become
barren.

A car driving down an unpaved path far to Duri's left
was causing the minor dust storm as it sped toward the
house. It had come from the direction of a major highway.
Soon the painted man, Mahmud, stepped out of the car,
followed by the driver. They exchanged a few words
before entering the house.

The general seemed content with the progress, first
checking his watch, then the direction of the highway.
More dust blew in, signaling the arrival of the next
contact—or so he thought. The truck barreling toward the
house carried four men, all armed with what appeared to
be AK-47 automatic rifles. Duri did not recognize the men
and now watched with heightened awareness.

The driver, hand picked for this mission, stepped onto
the porch alone and seemed to smile in the direction of the
intruders. Duri hoped that his expression was the result of
some sort of illusion formed by dust, distance, and
smudged binocular lenses. But he knew this was wishful
thinking.

The truck parked directly in front of the house and the
armed occupants piled out. The traitorous man standing on
the decrepit wooden porch stepped to the ground and
greeted them happily at the truck's front bumper. After

exchanging hearty handshakes and hugs, the five men circled and faced the truck. One of the militants set a briefcase on the hood and opened it, revealing a hefty sum of cash.

Duri focused on his traitor's smug expression and watched as the men entered the house. He snapped his pistol from its holster and checked his ammo. The Glock he wielded so effectively was definitely not standard Iraqi Army issue. Duri prized the weapon for its ability to withstand the dusty desert environment. The general had used it successfully many times and would again test its worth.

In a matter of minutes, he reached the side of the dilapidated farmhouse and peaked into the window of a back room. The tattooed soldier sat on the floor against the back wall, bound and gagged. Two of the armed men stood with the traitor in front of their prisoner, discussing the exchange.

The traitor set a portable lamp on the floor and flipped it on. The ambient light made it difficult to read, but the hidden markings were definitely there. With the confirmation, the traitor took his money, then left through the front after shaking the hands of the other two militants in the front room.

The leader of the group, Samir, reached down and lifted the prisoner to his feet. He had heard the front door close and an engine starting. But he had not heard the distinct sound of gravel crunching under tires. After nervously staring at the door, Samir turned to the second militant, Ghazi, and issued an order in his native tongue. "Why has he not gone yet? Go check."

Ghazi turned toward the door but stopped short when suddenly the car's engine revved loudly and gravel crackled. Then, in a blur of motion, the car crashed into the wooden porch and burst through the front wall. When he had regained his senses, Samir sent Ghazi out to investigate while he stayed with Mahmud, using the cowering prisoner as a human shield.

At the corner of the short central hallway, Ghazi pointed his AK-47 toward the gaping hole in the front wall of the house. The wooden timbers at the edge of the porch faltered, causing a section of the roof to cave in. The slow creaks and moans of cracking wood caused the gunman to step back, but the pile of rubble soon settled, leaving a dusty mess.

To his right, the traitor's car rested against the half wall separating the den from the kitchen. The engine continued groaning as the front tires spun slowly over the couch that propped up the vehicle. Another gunman lay pinned between the bumper and the ledge of the half wall. The gruesome sight turned his head, but Ghazi had no time to mourn. He feverishly scanned his surroundings, looking for an attacker. Instead, he found the fourth gunmen, another longtime friend, on the opposite side of the car—dead. Inside the car, a body laid still, his head propped up by the steering wheel. One bullet to the temple had finished him; the traitor never got the chance to spend his money.

Ghazi leaned in and checked the dead man's pulse, then backed away nervously. Nothing moved out front, but someone was out there, somewhere. He turned toward the hallway, intending to report to his leader.

The anxious gunman approached the back room carefully, swiveling his head in all directions. He paused when a pistol popped out from the kitchen's rear doorway to his left, taking him completely by surprise. The weapon fired three rounds, striking Ghazi high in the chest.

Samir watched through the doorway as his partner's body rocked violently with each impact, then collapsed to the floor. Samir crouched to a knee and shielded himself behind Mahmud's body. The barrel of his weapon dented the prisoner's cheek, as soft footsteps crept just to the right edge of the room's only door.

For a moment the lone gunman contemplated a rush for the window, but escaping without his prize would be out of the question. Then he thought how easily his bullets would penetrate the thin walls. He raised the rifle with one arm, working hard to steady his aim at the paneling just to the right of the doorway.

A burst of gunfire tore at the wall as General Duri spun into the opening with his pistol raised. The militant leader, keeping his finger pressed to the trigger, swept the rifle to the left. But Duri was too quick. With two shots to Samir's exposed head, the spray of bullets instantly darted ninety degrees upward, ending abruptly at the ceiling above Duri.

The dead man slumped awkwardly to the floor as the gunfire ended. Mahmud stood motionless with bulging eyes. This was the second time in two days that Duri had killed men within close proximity to him. After the shock wore off, he held up his bound hands, hoping to be freed. Duri holstered his weapon and obliged, cutting him loose.

The prisoner ripped the duct tape painfully from his mouth and spoke. "You've been following me?"

"Yes, I'm glad I did."

"Does this ruin the mission?"

"This was not part of the original plan, but the mission is still intact. I will adjust to this new development and you will reach your final destination."

Duri inspected the soldier for skin lesions, then did an odd thing. He leaned forward, causing Mahmud to recoil instinctively. Duri, sensing his fear, paused and smiled before kissing Mahmud on both cheeks. He was playing the fatherly role again, but Mahmud knew he could not trust this man. He had proven his complete lack of respect for human life twice during their short association. Mahmud backed away, lightly rubbing his cheeks.

"You are the last person on earth who should be afraid of me," said Duri. "Thank you for your loyalty to Iraq and your dedication to our cause."

Mahmud nodded humbly, wondering to what cause he had dedicated himself. The two men gathered a few extra weapons and exited through the gaping hole in the front of the house. They got into the truck outside and were soon racing toward the highway, leaving five more dead men in the dust.

Chapter Seven

Agent Naseth manned his rooftop post watching the storefront across the street. The center of the city remained relatively calm with much of the inhabitants either hiding in their houses or taking up defensive positions at the perimeter. Any movement on the street below could be quickly assessed without many distractions.

Naseth checked his watch and set down his binoculars in exchange for a canteen of water. He lay prone, peering just over the raised lip of the roof. During the middle part of the day he stayed in this position, waiting for the daily contact to arrive at the target house. At other times he set up near the center of the rooftop, under the shade of the access shed. There he used monitors linked to three small cameras he had installed at the roof's edge to keep an eye on the street below while monitoring coalition activities through the CIA computer network.

After finishing off his canteen, Naseth scowled, feeling as if someone were standing over him. He angled the metal canteen lid in his left hand to check for a reflection. As the dark image of a man filled the mirrored surface, he felt something brush against his left hip. Naseth flipped erratically to his back, fishing for his gun in a now empty holster. The man kneeling before him extended a weapon and pulled the trigger. A stream of water blasted Naseth directly in the face, causing him to flinch wildly.

Buzz laughed as Naseth cleared the water from his blurry eyes. "Hey, buddy. I brought you some more water just in case you ran out."

"Damn it, Buzz! Get down before someone sees you!"

Buzz handed his friend the sidearm he had taken and laid stomach to roof. "See, this is why analysts should stay in the office."

Naseth, still pissed, holstered his gun. "Where's your cowboy hat?"

"Left it back at the house. Didn't want anyone mistaking me for the President. Good to see you're still in one piece. I brought you the equipment you requested. But I don't know how you're going to get inside to bug the place."

"Hey, they sent me to Quantico for field training, and I've been on this assignment for a while now. I'm good."

"Yeah, I can tell. All the same, please allow me."

"Ah, don't you have to get back? I'm already getting tired of your sorry ass."

Buzz suddenly realized how he had missed his old friend's not so subtle wit. "Agent Reid and Colonel Blockhead are softening up my witness. Won't hurt to let them pound on him a while. By the time I get back, he'll think I'm his new best friend."

"But what about that palace? I bet it's pretty cozy."

"It's like Graceland, but much bigger. There's cheesy art everywhere, and gold-plated everything. I love it."

"I bet." Naseth slid backward and rose to a hunched stance. Buzz followed and they scurried to a bag sitting by the access shed. Naseth took inventory of the equipment that Buzz had brought, including the bugging equipment. He unpacked the tiny electronics like a kid on Christmas morning. "It's your show. How do we run this?"

Buzz handed him the empty canteen. "Looks like you're gonna need some more water."

* * *

Buzz stepped quietly past an overturned garbage bin at the end of a narrow alley. With an old dirty scarf wrapped across his face, no one would recognize him as American. He had the local attire down, all the way to his shoes. And a little dirt on the exposed portions of his skin took the shine off. The alleyway behind the store was clear, except for a skinny stray dog rummaging through the loose trash.

Fortunately for Buzz, the residence above the store had its own entrance serviced by a set of wooden stairs. He scanned his surroundings and slowly ascended the steps to a small concrete pad perched in front of a wooden door. He crouched with his back to the building, keeping an eye on the area below. He pressed the receiver a little deeper into his left ear and waited for his go-ahead signal.

Naseth casually crossed the gravelly street to the glass door he had been watching for weeks. With his Arab blood, a scarf was not needed to hide his face, so he kept his head wrap loosely draped over his shoulder and acted like he belonged in this besieged city.

The door was locked, as expected, and the front area looked clear. Naseth knocked loudly and grabbed the shoulder strap of the empty canteen. Inside, the suspected terrorist he had been monitoring stepped down from a set of stairs near the back room entrance. Naseth subtly turned his head and spoke into a concealed microphone at his wrist.

The suspect unlocked and slowly opened the door from the inside. Naseth presented the canteen and noticed a pistol in the suspect's right hand. In perfect Arabic, he questioned the anxious storeowner. "I'm sorry to bother you. I mean you no harm. My canteen is out of water, and

I have a good distance to walk before I get home. May I fill it with water? I will only be a minute."

The man smiled and lowered the gun. "Are you working with the rebels fighting the British?"

Naseth thought momentarily. "No, I do not believe in violence, but I do hope the occupiers leave soon. I do not want them in my country."

The suspect nodded and moved aside. "Good. Come inside and you may have your water. It is no problem."

One story above, Buzz picked the lock and entered the small residence. It consisted of a small kitchenette, a small living area, and a single bedroom. A set of stairs descended from an opening at the opposite wall. He worked quietly and methodically, listening to the conversation in his earpiece while planting bugs in each room. He used an especially sensitive device behind the railing at the top of the stairs that would easily pick up voices from anywhere on the lower level.

Buzz left through the door and crept down the wooden stairs to the alley below. He rounded the building to the front and ambled across the storefront, looking around like he was lost. Naseth emerged from the back room and acknowledged his partner through the glass. He thanked the gracious host and exited with his full canteen, brushing past his partner on his way out. The two went their separate ways, hoping to see each other soon in friendlier surroundings.

Chapter Eight

The guns had mostly quieted by nightfall in the southern sector of the Radwaniyah Presidential Palace complex. The soldiers had unofficially renamed their new base Camp Slayer and had cleared out the last defenders from the complex. The airport was now mostly under coalition control as well. Soon, American airplanes would begin landing at the airport, bringing fresh troops and supplies.

Agent Reid and Colonel Block tag-teamed their wily informant, Lieutenant Hashimi, inside the interrogation room. He had already told them about Mahmud escaping through the tunnel, but they were convinced he knew more than he let on. Army scouts had already investigated the first contact location, but had apparently showed up too late. The tunnel exit at the northern outskirts of the city of Ar Ramadi had already been opened from the inside and hastily covered. But Hashimi claimed he had no idea where the target had gone from there, nor what valuable information the man carried with him.

Block was growing tired of the prisoner's double talk and ordered Lieutenant Sedal to monitor his vitals using sophisticated lie detection equipment in the observation room. So far, Sedal had indicated Hashimi could be telling the truth, which frustrated the colonel even more.

After a long pause in the questioning, Block tried again. "OK, I'm going to ask you in a different way." He moved in close to Hashimi, who was seated on the opposite side of the table. "Tell me about the driver who picked up this Mahmud Jafari in Ramadi. How was he chosen for this mission?"

Block stood behind him, casting a huge shadow, but the tactic did not intimidate the prisoner.

"I think he was chosen by the hand of God himself," said Hashimi.

Block despised sarcasm. Reid could see it in his eyes and moved in. By the time she reached the men, Block had jerked Hashimi from the chair and thrown him to the ground. "I'm through playing games!"

Reid slipped in between the men, palms to the colonel's chest. "Come on, if he were lying, the equipment would have picked it up. Let's take a break."

"Good idea!" Buzz exclaimed from the doorway. "Let me take it." He strode around the other end of the table as Reid ushered the fuming colonel out of the room. Buzz helped the handcuffed prisoner to his feet and straightened his ruffled shirt. "You OK?"

"I'm fine. I have been treated much worse." He motioned to the scar on the right side of his neck that extended down to his shoulder.

"I guess so. Can I get you something? Water? I got a few boxes of those clove cigarettes you mentioned earlier."

Hashimi smiled as he took his seat. "That would be good. I take one now."

Buzz opened a new pack and handed Hashimi a cigarette. After lighting it, he poured water and set the glass in front of his new friend. "So, I guess they treated you rough while I was gone. Sorry about that. Colonel Block just isn't a patient man."

"That's OK. As long as the girl is here, I'm OK."

Reid smirked from behind the glass.

Buzz gave Hashimi a friendly pat on the back. "I know what you mean. Anyway, I'll try not to throw you to the wolves like that again."

Hashimi blew smoke and looked confused. "I do not get this expression."

Buzz, now casually walking around the table, realized he would have to watch his idioms. "Oh, I mean leaving you to get eaten. Block is the big wolf."

"Ah, I get it. You Americans have so many expressions. I sometimes have watched your TV shows and I do not understand everything. I hear the laughing, but do not know what they are laughing at."

"I didn't think you got American television here in Iraq. Guess that's why you speak such good English."

"Yes, I think I like your cop shows best. They always have good cop and bad cop. In Iraq, we only have bad cop, and very bad cop."

Buzz paused and faked a smile. "So, you think I'm playing the good cop?"

"Yes, but I like the good cop."

Buzz ducked his head and shuffled through the file on the table. He found a picture and slid it across to Hashimi, giving him a moment to study. "Well, now that we understand each other, let's see if you can help me out. I still think you're a good guy. I'm not acting when I say that."

Hashimi studied the photograph for a moment, then looked at Buzz. "Sorry, I do not recognize this man." His expression changed subtly from pleasant, to concerned.

Buzz reached up and seemed to push at something in his left ear, then nodded. "They tell me you're not being completely honest with me. I really thought we could trust each other, but I guess that was just wishful thinking," Buzz said, feigning disappointment.

Hashimi nervously scanned the room, noticing the cameras and mirrored glass. Considering the opulent surroundings, it was easy for Hashimi to forget the technology being used against him. He decided to hold his cards a little closer to the vest. "I think you are bluffing. They could not know if I am telling the truth."

"Come on. You said you watched our cop shows. Those cameras feed a close-up image of your eyes to a computer. The software on the computer can measure small retinal movements in your eye. They can measure all kinds of things from in there. You lied to me."

Hashimi buried his face in his hands. Although he did not fully grasp the technical terms in English, he understood that he had been caught. "I am sorry my friend. This is not personal. I only fear for my life if I tell you all I know."

"If you're talking about Saddam's security forces, then I wouldn't be too concerned with them. You are protected. They can't get to you."

"I hear the bombs and guns outside all the time. You cannot protect me if you cannot even protect yourself."

"You're not afraid to die. You're afraid of being tortured. I know how hard it is for you to believe, but the leaders of Iraq are no longer in control of this country. They can't get to you anymore. Believe me."

Hashimi stubbed the cigarette in the ashtray and glanced at the mirror again. "I tell you, but not in here. We go for a walk outside and I tell you. We will test your defenses."

"I'm not too sure the colonel's going to let that happen."

"This is the only way I say a thing."

Buzz looked toward the observation room and waited for a response. Finally, Block's voice boomed through the earpiece, giving him permission to take the prisoner. Buzz turned to Hashimi, who was already anxiously standing by the door.

As they walked past the observation room, Block stood in the hallway, staring Hashimi down. He despised the little man. But he loathed the fact that the CIA would interview him off record even more.

Chapter Nine

Buzz led the handcuffed prisoner out through a back door and across a stone walkway. The path ended at the concrete fortified bank of the Tigris River. Hashimi breathed deep, taking in the smell of the brisk night. He had not been outside in several days, and the fresh open air assaulted his senses.

Buzz stood beside him, enjoying the break from his long day. After several minutes of silence, he leaned in and grabbed Hashimi's hands. Suddenly, the cuffs slid apart, freeing the prisoner's arms.

"Thank you." Hashimi rubbed his sore wrists and motioned to the box in Buzz's shirt pocket. In seconds, Hashimi was puffing on another clove cigarette and stretching his arms. Behind them, the sounds of war thumped like a distant fireworks show. Some of the abbreviated small arms fire had to be within a mile of the palace.

"Those guns are a little too close, if you ask me."

Hashimi agreed, peering through the darkness, looking for tracer fire. "You know, Buzz, I would not get too comfortable here."

"What do you mean?"

"I have very good reason to be afraid. The Republican Guard does not need to communicate with Saddam. The units are trained to break into small mortar teams as defense positions get destroyed. Then they fight like hit and run. Very hard to find and very dangerous. They can hit us right here."

"You mean guerrilla warfare? I'm sure our military is ready for that."

"We will see about this."

"Maybe they'll just give up and go home like the regulars did."

"I think not. The Guard soldiers are very loyal. The commanders have all authority now. Do not need orders from generals anymore."

Buzz watched the red streaks, now getting closer to the camp's northern checkpoints. "So there's a bunch of well-trained and well-armed jackrabbits out there getting ready to hit us with mortars."

Hashimi chuckled. "These jackrabbits may be across the river aiming right now at us."

"Good thing I got us out of the building, then. Safer out here." Another long silence followed as they monitored the sights and sounds. "So, why are you helping the CIA? You just told me how loyal Republican Guard soldiers are."

Hashimi thought about the question carefully. "Not all of us are in love with Saddam. General Duri knows this. He is smart. That is why I know little of this plan."

"Maybe he planned for you to get captured all along. And he sensed you weren't the most loyal soldier. So maybe he intended for you to tell us certain things to throw us off. Considering how this was planned, I wouldn't rule it out."

"Yes, it is very possible. I hope you catch him and put him in my jail cell." Hashimi was now visibly upset. Buzz had hit a nerve.

"Easy now. That's why we're out here. You ready to tell me who the man in that picture is?"

"He is an official in Basrah. I see him visit the General a few times. Last week he comes two times."

"What did they talk about?"

"They are like good friends, these two. They talk about meeting a foreign contact about something."

"So why all this set up with the soldier and the General escaping through a tunnel? Sounds like too much trouble. Why not just have this official give the information directly to the contact?"

"We do not even know what information."

"I think it has something to do with weapons of mass destruction."

"We do not call them that, but this is what I think. I hear the General talk of these weapons."

"Did he mention terrorists?"

"I hear him speak of al Qaeda sometimes, but not too much."

A pitched battle now raged to the north, in the direction of the bridge. Both men kept an eye to the north as tanks rolled in that direction from the east.

"So what's this official's name?"

"Sayf Muhammad Said al Tikriti."

"You guys need shorter names."

The joke did not register with Hashimi. To him, their names were of perfectly normal length. A man's name represents parts of his lineage and includes tribal references. He realized that Buzz probably did not understand, so he let the comment go without argument.

Buzz closely monitored his informant's body language to ensure he did not cross any religious or cultural boundaries. With his last feeble attempt at a joke, he sensed Hashimi's annoyance.

"So, what about this meeting? Could it be one of the contacts the escaped soldier, uh, Mahmud is looking for?"

"If so, it will be soon. What is today?"

"It's after 11:00 on April 4th."

"The meeting is planned for tomorrow night after the sun goes down. But I think it is the General, not Mahmud. He says he will see him there."

"That's good enough for me. I'll take what I can get. Does he know you heard him setting up this meeting?"

"He did not hide it, but he did not know I was near him."

"Hmm, sounds a little suspicious, but we have to check it out." Buzz let him crush out the cigarette before applying the cuffs. As he again secured the prisoner, Buzz schemed, "Where is this meeting?"

"West of Al Kut. First bridge before the first buildings of the city."

"OK, you'll get some extra stuff out of this. What do you want?"

"Ice box."

"A refrigerator? Good, I'll get it stocked full of beer. Just act like you haven't told me anything yet. I don't want Block in on this."

"I like this plan. But I am sorry; I do not drink beer. Coca Cola."

"You got it. Now let's get inside before we get shot."

Chapter Ten

Buzz met Reid in their office and revealed his findings. She agreed to withhold the information from Block pending further cooperation on the Army's part. Her primary orders originated directly from the Oval Office, so she felt her authority lay outside their chain-of-command anyway.

Reid began tapping the keys on her laptop. "Let's contact Naseth about this and have him follow Sayf to the meeting. We'll be ready at the bridge as backup." She found the secure server she was looking for and located Naseth's login. He was watching for message posts as expected, so she relayed the new information and waited for a response.

It took some time for the data to traverse the network of landlines and satellites. Minutes later, Naseth posted his reply. Another visitor had come to the hideout hours earlier, and this time Naseth had recorded the conversation. Parts of the discussion confirmed the meeting, but there were no specifics as to what prize awaited these terrorists. Before logging off, Naseth uploaded the digital recordings for Reid to analyze.

"Looks like your bugs worked. Naseth will know to follow Sayf, and we'll have to work out a way to monitor the hideout."

"Don't worry about that. Naseth will take care of it. He's pretty sharp."

"Smarter than you?"

"Well yeah, but not nearly as handsome."

Reid laughed a little too loudly as they started reviewing files and conducting research on Sayf. But they would not get the opportunity to settle in. Block rudely interrupted, returning Reid the favor from earlier. The agents shielded their computer screens by standing awkwardly by their desks.

The giant zeroed in on Buzz. "Well, are you going to report your findings to me? I extended you the courtesy of taking my prisoner on a nature walk, and you don't even share your conversation with me?"

Reid stepped in. "You still don't get it. He's not your prisoner. And he is the key witness in an investigation that the President has given me full authority to conduct. That means I am in charge of what happens to Hashimi, and any information we get from him."

Block was losing his grip on the investigation. Reid was right. Basically, she was in charge, and her power came directly from his commander-in-chief. Any problems he caused the CIA would amount to insubordination, which would be a good way to end his career.

Buzz put his hand lightly on Reid's shoulder. "That's OK agent Reid. Colonel, I'm sorry I didn't come to you first. I just thought you'd want a written report."

Block appreciated Buzz helping him save face. His honor was very important to him, and Buzz had just shown him the respect he felt he deserved. "Thank you agent Foster. I would like a written report for the record, as well as a verbal summary if you would be so kind."

Again, Buzz had played good cop. He led Block to the door and spoke softly. Reid sat silently at her desk.

"I didn't get much information from Hashimi," Buzz said. "He says he knows the man in the picture, but won't talk yet."

Block considered this. "What do we need to get him to talk? How can we motivate him?"

"He asked for a refrigerator full of Cokes for starters."

Block laughed and slapped Buzz on the shoulder. "He's getting smarter. First he asks for a house, and now we're down to an appliance. He'll have it as soon as I can get a requisition in. One of these mansions ought to have an icebox somewhere."

"Good. I think he wants to help, but he's being a little greedy. Why not improve his accommodations while you're at it?"

Just as they were concluding, Lieutenant Sedal stepped in the doorway. "Hi Buzz, agent Reid. I set up a secure space on our server. Here's your protocol." He handed Buzz a folder and started to leave.

"Colonel, I'm going to get some sleep, if it's OK with you," Sedal said.

"Hold on a minute. There's something I wanted to discuss." Block shook hands with Buzz, then followed the lieutenant into the hallway, closing the door behind him.

Sedal was wondering why the colonel's mood had suddenly changed from jovial to serious. "What's wrong?"

Block held a finger up to his mouth and ushered Sedal down the hall. "I want you to find out anything they may be hiding from me—especially information from Hashimi. They must keep records of reports and contacts on their laptops. And monitor their communications with Langley. Anything you can find, copy it."

"Sir, you're asking me to spy on CIA agents and possibly hack into the CIA computer system?"

Block squinted. "Yes, Lieutenant. Any problems with that?"

A smile emerged on Sedal's lips. "No sir. Just wanted to be clear."

* * *

The early morning sun beat down on Mahmud as he loaded crates onto a small flat boat tethered to the bank of the Tigris River. Over the previous two days, he had taken a looping clockwise path to his current location south of the Lake Tharthar palace, where he had started the journey. Baghdad lay further south, and he would soon travel through the coalition-controlled capital.

Mahmud climbed the sharp slope of the riverbank, slipping on the pebbles and loose dirt. He found the last crate in the back of the truck and paused to wipe his brow, enjoying the shade from the trees. But he dared not rest too long with the General nearby, possibly watching. Duri had set a strict schedule to follow.

Minutes later, Mahmud pulled the cord on the tiny engine, which sputtered to life. The boat slowly edged away from land and soon merged with the main flow of the river, heading south. It did not take long to run into trouble. An American marine patrol lay in wait up ahead, their Humvee parked on a flat segment of the river bank.

A soldier stepped onto the soft ground and motioned to Mahmud. He would have to stop, but had no reason to worry. The boat carried nothing to concern the U.S. military, at least not anything they could see.

General Duri watched from a distance upstream. He wedged his two-man johnboat against a sandbar near a meander in the river and grabbed a cane fishing pole. As the situation progressed, Duri let the red and yellow bob float freely, without bait. Through his binoculars, he could see Mahmud pleading his case to the American, even opening his crates to reveal the harmless contents of fruits and vegetables.

Then, smiling humbly, he offered a ripe melon to the soldier. A nice touch, thought Duri. It worked. The soldier cheerfully accepted the fruit and sent the honest, hard-working Iraqi citizen on his way. As the boat drifted into the main current at the center of the river, the soldier waved and split the melon into four pieces. Three other soldiers soon joined him at the front of the vehicle.

Duri pulled in his fishing line and fired up the engine. The tiny boat rounded the meander and joined the heavier flow of the straightaway. The soldiers seemed content to let him pass without challenge, even waving, trying to make friends with the locals. Duri simultaneously respected them as soldiers and despised them for the country they represented. Still, he returned the greeting as he drifted past, just another harmless Iraqi citizen.

The flat boat carrying Mahmud stayed mostly within sight, temporarily hiding in the twists and turns of the river. Each of the men settled in for the journey. Baghdad lay ahead and their destiny awaited somewhere beyond.

Chapter Eleven

A chemist working with the CIA grabbed the last page
of her first official analysis performed in Iraq. She hoped
it would produce some sort of earth-shattering, or at least
case-breaking, information for the agents in country. Buzz
took the papers, promising to keep her informed. He
stepped out of the tiny mobile lab onto the grounds of a
busy motor pool, oblivious to the swarms of men and
vehicular traffic around him.

The palace headquarters stood a short distance away.
Buzz read while walking a meandering path in that
general direction, nearly tripping over the perfectly
manicured hedges lining the front driveway. As he
regained his balance, laughter drifted from the palace's
main doors. Reid had stopped under the *porte-cochere*,
apparently on her way out, before witnessing her partner's
clumsiness.

"You think that's funny, huh?"

"I just can't seem to match the man with his service
record."

Buzz approached, still slightly embarrassed. "Guess I
let my guard down a little knowing I'm surrounded by
U.S. soldiers. Where're you headed?" He handed her the
papers he'd been so fixated on.

Reid gave them a cursory review. "Oh, just thought I'd
get some fresh air. I haven't seen much of the river. So
what's the summary on this?"

"The chemist basically said the bulbs would produce a
unique light spectrum with the amount of voltage I told
her we were estimating. She thinks it could be used to pick
up certain pigments, like a black light does. We're talking

about a light spectrum that's not used, at least not commercially. But it wouldn't be too hard to come up with something like this."

"So it was probably developed as a proprietary device. Government funded research. They could have created a special pigment to use in conjunction with the light, something for hidden messages."

"It's the only thing I can figure. The chemist ruled it out as a medical device."

Reid moved away from the door, walking and talking. "OK, here's a theory. They knew going in that the coalition would overrun the Iraqi Army. Their electronic communications would be severed. High command would have a hard time keeping in touch with foot soldiers. But if they planned to continue waging a guerrilla war, they would need a new way to give orders. Maybe this is how they are supposed to communicate."

Reid motioned for Buzz to follow as she walked south, toward the corner of the building. Buzz kept up. "We're saying they would use hidden messages written in a special invisible ink that could only be read by a specific type of light?"

"That's my theory."

Reid turned right at the corner and headed toward the river.

"Hashimi mentioned the army might break into small mortar teams to continue fighting guerrilla style. He even said they wouldn't need to stay in contact with the high command. But I can't see every single one of these little units carrying around a bulky light fixture, even if they had that many. This is starting to seem a little farfetched.

It would take a lot of advanced planning for something like this."

"But they expected us to eventually attack them. We spent billions to plan for all kind of contingencies."

"True."

"Maybe they planned to send the messages out to predetermined rendezvous locations already set up with these light units. They, in turn, relay orders or intelligence to these quasi-independent units through other means."

"I still think there has to be a much simpler explanation."

They reached the concrete embankment at the river's edge, with Reid fanning herself in the searing heat. She removed her blouse, revealing a white form-fitting camisole, showing off her toned physique. Buzz did not mind the heat, and he certainly had no problem with getting a better look at Reid.

"You better watch out, you might offend the locals showing that much skin."

Reid was a little more feminine and flirtatious than usual. "You want me to cover up? I don't see any Iraqis."

"I guess you have the right to get some sun. Who am I to stop you?"

Reid stretched, heaving her chest, teasing Buzz. "I'm glad you're willing to put up with it."

Buzz couldn't help staring. "Are you having fun torturing me?"

"Actually, yes I am."

"I'm sure there are rules against this kind of thing," Buzz said.

Reid gave him a lingering look, then got back to business. "Naseth reported that the target house had a visitor. He brought the subject a package. From what he could hear, it's some sort of reading device. Goes well with our theory. If we can intercept him tonight, we'll have an intact device, and a man who knows what to use it for."

"That would help explain things. It could also lead us right to the General and the other missing soldier."

"I'm going to think about how to plan this raid tonight without including Block. I'll coordinate with Naseth to make sure he'll be in position."

"And me?"

"Well, since you're all work and no play, I want you to take another look at the equipment found in the surgical room."

"Yes, boss."

"And find out who the fourth dead guy was."

"The one that wasn't a doctor? Yes ma'am." He tipped his hat and started to leave. Before he could, Reid placed a hand lightly on his stomach. "To answer your question from earlier, the only rules I care to follow are the ones that affect our mission. Anything else is nobody's business but ours."

"You're the boss."

Buzz clasped her hand in his, gazing down into her gleaming brown eyes. They broke contact, then he turned and strode away. Reid watched him closely before turning back to the river.

Chapter Twelve

Agent Andrew Sumner poked his head around the corner of an old building and scanned a market in the Kurdish-controlled town of Agrah. The plaza, an intersection of narrow gravel roads, bustled with activity in the early afternoon sun. The locals seemed oblivious to the problems facing the southern portions of their country. The only visible signs of a new Iraqi era came from a small contingent of U.S. soldiers that had established a base to the south of town. The Kurds were happy to accommodate, knowing they would be protected from Saddam and his brutal army.

Sumner kept his white skin covered with dirt and clothes. Even though Americans were mostly welcome in the town, his current assignment required discretion. Agent Reid had contacted him regarding a suspected foreign terrorist hideout located in Agrah. Naseth had heard some chatter, indicating his subject would link up with the Kurdish cell somewhere in town. But that was all he knew. He would have to find the location of the hideout himself.

The generalities of the operation were enough for an agent of Sumner's stature to proceed. With Reid's authorization, he had spent most of the last twelve hours paying off Kurds for information on anyone who did not belong in the village. Like any small town, everyone knew everyone else. Outsiders were easily spotted and watched closely. It did not take long to find the foreigners, and most of the town's citizens would have helped the CIA for free. Sumner had watched the hideout for most of the day, gathering information. His instincts told him the terrorists were getting ready to make their next move.

Sumner followed the only two members of the Kurdish terrorist cell he had identified as they ventured out for their mid-day meal. He had help from a Special Forces soldier he borrowed from an outpost south of town.

A gung-ho Army Ranger Specialist, Darin Helton had volunteered for the mission, apparently itching for some action. The unusual request was granted, though Helton's commander had reservations. He did not like the idea of one of his men entering a murky situation without much support. But intelligence resources were limited in the war on terror, so, fortunately for Sumner, the commander had decided to grant the request.

The two suspects Sumner now tracked waded through a group of children playing on the opposite corner of the plaza. They had found a fruit and vegetable stand, bought some produce and flatbread, then searched for a place to sit and eat. The two men found a suitable bench under an awning at the opposite side of the plaza.

Sumner positioned himself more to his left to get a better view, and to present himself to Helton. He signaled by yawning and stretching his arms. His partner had blended into the marketplace well, and Sumner could only find him when his signal was answered. Helton had situated himself next to another set of benches near the suspects. They were eating their lunch, only a stone's throw from an alley entrance.

Sumner was wondering if Helton could hear them talking from his position when he quickly realized a failure in planning the surveillance operation. He had no idea whether Helton could speak any of the languages the suspects would be using. He quietly cursed himself for the oversight. The locals had mentioned the two strangers spoke Arabic, but the older of the two was clearly Iranian. The younger man had only arrived the previous day, so Sumner had little information about him. Either way, it was a pretty good bet that they would probably not be speaking English.

Unexpectedly, the two men wrapped up their half-eaten food and walked briskly in Helton's direction. Sumner could see him make eye contact with the men before they took a quick right into the alley, disappearing from view only a few steps from the sidewalk. Sumner had conducted many of these operations, and had developed an instinct for situations turning bad. It seemed to him that Helton had been identified. His new partner apparently had not blended in as well as he had previously thought.

Sumner tried to call the operation off, signaling to Helton, who was now peeking down the alley. After a quick look around, he ignored Sumner and vanished around the corner.

Helton stepped quietly through the dirt, trying to find his suspects. But the low sun was casting a blinding glare. He stopped, shielding his eyes behind the edge of the next building, which jutted further into the alley than the rest.

In the shadows, Helton could make out the fuzzy form of the younger suspect. He could not see the second man, though. He determined that he needed a better vantage point, and the opposite side of the alley looked promising. The uneven walls on that side would also provide suitable hiding places. He waited for the younger man to move into the sun, then darted efficiently across to a nook.

This angle improved his view tremendously, but Helton still could not locate the second suspect. He would have to move forward to keep up, but his instincts nagged at him. He kept close to the wall, briskly jogging toward the next nook. Before Helton reached the corner, he stopped at a door and slowly shook the handle. It was locked, so he moved forward to a wooden staircase that led to a second-story entrance.

Helton was very close to the younger man now, and the staircase provided sufficient cover. But soon, the suspects would be running out of the alley, which made the situation very tenuous. The younger man had stopped about fifteen meters past the staircase, and was stretching his arms. His partner had to be close, and Helton smelled a trap. He stood to a crouch, and turned back toward the locked door.

Without warning, the older man thrust a knife at Helton's side, its darting blade gleaming in a sliver of sunlight. But Helton was quicker. In a single motion, he sidestepped the weapon with a smooth pivot and grabbed the attacker's forearm, twisting it hard to the left. A follow-up thrust from his right arm caught the man square in the throat, slamming him into the wall with brute force.

Helton heard the shuffle of feet from behind and dropped the older man's limp body in order to draw his sidearm. The younger man managed to fire a flailing shot from a small handgun before Helton turned full circle. The old man yelled at his partner in Arabic as Helton stepped out from behind the stairs to get a better aim. The younger gunman had already started his escape before Helton could get off his first return volley. Three quick shots rang out, splintering wood and chipping clay walls, but missing their mark as the suspect rounded the corner.

Sumner sprinted into the alley at the other end and could see Helton firing at someone darting around the far corner. He ran as fast as he could toward Helton, with his weapon drawn. Then, through the blur of the sun, another figure emerged from the shadows. Sumner almost screamed a warning, but it was too late. The older man had gotten to his feet, and with a quick jerking thrust, plunged a knife into Helton's back. Sumner heard a loud sickening groan.

"Shit!" Sumner spat, then he pulled up into a firing position and squeezed off three rapid rounds. The wood splintered off the stairs as the suspect ducked. He grabbed Helton's pistol off the ground and returned fire while running backwards. The wild shots posed little threat, and Sumner walked steadily into the gunfire, emptying his magazine.

His juggernaut-like advance unnerved the older man, who turned tail and ran. Although at this distance he had trouble effectively hitting a moving target, Sumner managed to hit the suspect in the arm with his last shot. He could hear the older man's screams trail off around the corner of the building, as he followed the younger man and made his escape.

Sumner reached Helton, who was lying bent in a pool of his own blood. He frantically ripped the soldier's shirt and tumbled Helton onto his side. As Sumner compressed the wound with wads of blood-soaked clothing, Helton turned his head toward him. In a labored grunt, he whispered, "I'm sorry, I broke contact—pretty stupid."

Sumner realized it was hopeless, so he scooted through the pool of blood on both knees and carefully laid him on his back. Helton had gone completely limp.

"Agent Sumner," Helton rasped. "The older one was protecting the younger man."

"I think you hit him before he got away," Sumner lied. "I'll find him."

Helton smiled. "Good. Get that other bastard too."

Sumner did his best to make Helton comfortable, using his own shirt as a pillow. He could see the pride in Helton's eyes, and searched his heart for encouraging words. "You did a great service to your country. I didn't tell you before, but that man you shot is very important. That's why the other one was protecting him. Now that he's wounded, we'll follow his blood trail, which will lead us right to him."

"If I get a medal, I want my brother to have it," Helton whispered.

Sumner clasped his hand and squeezed tightly. "I'll make sure of it. Your brother will get that medal, I promise."

Helton's broad smile faded as his grip loosened. Sumner removed his dog tags and unlatched the satellite phone from his own belt. He stared into the dead man's frozen eyes for a moment, trying to imagine a scenario that would garner a posthumous commendation. As far as anyone else was concerned, Helton had died heroically for his country.

A better version of the incident formed in his mind. The military outpost was only twenty minutes away, so he would leave the body to be picked up. He dialed the numbers that would inform command as to the location, then dragged Helton's corpse out of sight under the staircase. He did not have the luxury of sticking around to explain, or to wait for new clothes, for that matter. Sumner was determined to bring some sort of meaning to Helton's death. And finding the two missing terrorists would honor him more than any medal.

Chapter Thirteen

Reid disconnected her satellite phone and stared out through the CIA office door. She could see the window in the opposite room, and thought how peaceful the world seemed through that tiny porthole. Buzz leaned on his desk, waiting for her to process the bad news she had just been told. He had heard enough to understand the basic problem they now faced, but needed her to fill in the gaps.

Reid took a deep breath, then turned her sad eyes to Buzz. "The man who died was Specialist Darin Helton. He was an Army Ranger tapped by one of our agents to do surveillance on a high-priority group of foreigners working out of Agrah. It's a village in Kurdish territory. One of the Arab suspects killed him while trying to protect another man. Agent Sumner is trying to reacquire the two suspects."

"What about a description? Sounds like it fits the scenario of our two missing Iraqis, not foreign terrorists," Buzz remarked.

"Helton sent photos, and we're trying to identify them now. We can't confirm they're foreigners or Iraqis yet."

"They'll assume they were followed, so they'll be looking for a new hideout. Sumner may need help tracking them," Buzz said.

"Well, the older suspect was wounded protecting the younger one, so Sumner will be able to pick up a blood trail. We'll deal with the suspects we're tracking tonight. Once we have a better idea of the situation, we'll determine if we can spare you to help Sumner. He may not need us," Reid said.

61

Buzz thought for a moment, then seemed aggravated for the first time since Reid had met him. "If these men turn out to be the real targets, then Hashimi lied to us."

Reid nodded. She shared his concern, but did not get the chance to respond. A strange machine appeared in the doorway, immediately drawing their attention. The contraption looked like an overgrown remote-controlled car, with a thick metal platform over tracks instead of wheels. The crude machine propelled itself toward the agents. Buzz warily leaned in to investigate.

The robot stopped, then unfolded a metal arm from the top of its platform. The end of the probe reached chest level before Buzz realized what was going on. There was a black box at the end of the arm that appeared to house a camera.

Buzz cracked a broad grin in Reid's direction. Then the arm retracted as Lieutenant Sedal strolled through the door holding a large remote control. "Hey Buzz. Like my new toy?"

"Yes, Lieutenant. Had me wonderin' there for a minute."

"Did you see the camera on the arm? They used these babies in Afghanistan to go into the caves. They're called PackBots."

"I'm used to CIA gadgets. They're small and sleek. This is just an overgrown movie camera," Buzz said.

Sedal seemed to deflate a little, glancing down at the remote in his hands as if it were last year's model. "Well, that's about all this one is, that's true. It's the basic model. But they have dozens of versions that can do everything from launch a smoke grenade to open doors with a second arm. They've even worked on one that uses a USB port to hack into computers."

"Now that's more like it," Buzz said. "When're you bringing one of those in?"

"I haven't seen the other versions yet, but they sound pretty cool."

Reid eyed the PackBot, shook her head, and left the geeks to their tech talk. She had a situation out in the field that was spinning out of control, a dead ranger, and two suspects on the run who might hold the key to WMDs. She needed to think.

Sedal watched her leave, then handed Buzz the remote. "Why don't you keep this one for now? Play around with it if you want; I'll be back for it in a day or two."

"Thanks. I'll try to keep it in one piece."

"Good idea not to be tinkering with it. Even though it's pretty basic, it cost a bundle. I don't think you could afford to pay for the damages."

Sedal glanced at the robot one last time in a way that seemed a little odd to Buzz, then left. Buzz half-heartedly played with the PackBot, guiding it by watching the small monitor on the remote, but his mind was elsewhere. He absently placed the remote on his desk, then decided to go in search of Reid. She already had a head start getting access to Hashimi, but he looked forward to grilling the Iraqi himself about the two men in Agrah. They had already killed one man, but they could be the conduit for the mass murder of thousands if those WMDs ever found their way into the wrong hands.

* * *

Sedal entered the main computer room near the kitchen just as Reid walked out. He signaled Block with a nod, and they checked the perimeter of the room to ensure they were alone. Block flipped on his computer, then gave it to Sedal. Soon a video feed showing the inside of the CIA office popped on the screen. The lieutenant used the keyboard to bring the PackBot to life. With a few taps, the arm extended fully, and the PackBot rolled toward Reid's computer. Sedal grabbed a joystick, like the ones that might otherwise be used for video games, and began manipulating the machine.

Another arm appeared at the bottom of the video feed and extended over the keyboard. With a few more keystrokes, he had a bird's eye view of Reid's keyboard. A minute later, he had the second extension plugged into the USB port on the side of the laptop.

Block watched in amazement as Sedal minimized the video feed window and pulled up the system files. After some hacking, every piece of information on Reid's computer had been transferred to Army Intelligence.

Block patted Sedal on the back. "Good job, Lieutenant. Get a few men to help you sift through recent files concerning this investigation. Start from now and work backwards. Let me know immediately if there is anything important that we don't already know."

"Yes, sir."

Block exited as Sedal returned the PackBot to its previous place, making it look as if it had never moved. It would not take long for him to find a report detailing the upcoming meeting between the escaped general and a provincial official near al Kut.

* * *

Buzz and Reid gazed into the dark hallway toward the stockade's holding cells as an MP escorted Hashimi to the front of the building. The prisoner seemed happy to get out, but his mood changed upon seeing the agents' somber faces. He stepped into the small front room and presented his cuffs to the guard. Buzz shook his head at the MP, signaling to him to leave Hashimi secured. Then Buzz angrily grabbed the prisoner's upper arm and forcefully led him out of the building to the open space of the courtyard.

Reid followed, leaning in to whisper a warning to her partner. "Careful, we still want Block to think you guys are buddies."

Buzz nodded, then loosened his grip and smiled through clenched teeth. They decided to ferry Hashimi far away from prying ears and headed for their favorite riverfront spot. When Buzz got to the river, he released Hashimi by shoving him rudely to the water's edge. The prisoner turned, eyes wide, deep furrows sculpting his brow. "I do not understand this."

Buzz took a deep breath. "Are you enjoying your nice cold sodas, Hashimi?"

"Yes, very much. Thank you for that my friend."

Reid stepped forward, diverting his attention from Buzz. "He's not your friend, Hashimi. He's mad because you lied to him. Friends don't lie to each other."

Hashimi seemed to search his memory, as if he could not possibly find anything he had said to deceive Buzz. "What did I lie? I tell you the General is meeting that man tonight. You will see."

Buzz forced his way back into the conversation. "What do you know about Agrah?"

"Agrah is Kurdish. We have nothing to do there."

"One of our soldiers was killed there while tracking suspected terrorists. An older man was protecting a younger man. Sound like a familiar scenario?"

"Iraqi soldiers are not terrorists. If they are foreigners, we have nothing to do with them."

"As far as you know," Reid said.

"That is true. I tell you what I know. I know what I hear or what the General tells me. I hear nothing about a plan in Kurdish areas. Only in al Kut, this night."

Buzz wasn't ready to buy the whole act, but he realized Hashimi could be telling the truth. He had only been given bits and pieces of the overall plan, so maybe he had not purposely misled them. "You know, Reid, it's possible the group in Agrah are just decoys."

"Or, maybe they aren't even related to this operation," Reid suggested. "We haven't positively identified them as our missing Iraqis yet. Could be they really are foreigners."

Hashimi offered a third possibility. "Maybe the General and Mahmud are the decoys."

The agents slowly turned to him as if he had just found the cure for cancer. "I guess we'll find out for sure tonight," Reid responded.

Buzz exhaled, giving Hashimi a sideways glance, then patted him on the back, gently prodding him back to the stockade.

Block was waiting just outside Hashimi's cell, hoping for new information. Apparently, he would have to get it

by other means. As he had expected, Buzz was
stonewalling him again.

Chapter Fourteen

General Duri stood at the center of a grove of trees and used his night vision binoculars to watch Mahmud's flat boat drift lazily downstream. The General had left his johnboat as they neared al Kut so he could take the high ground. From the river embankment, he could monitor the next contact and have the flexibility to intercede if needed. Considering the fiasco at the farmhouse, Duri stayed alert.

Mahmud's boat entered a curve in the river ahead and drifted to the left. Duri had scouted this meander months earlier and knew it would loop back around before straightening again. Soon after, Mahmud would find an inlet where his next contact was waiting.

Duri watched until the boat disappeared from view, then he cut across the loop and found another grove of trees to hide in. He did not wait long before the boat rounded the corner and headed directly toward his position. Now he turned his attention downstream, looking for signs of trouble. A good distance ahead, the river split, making it hard for Duri to see what was going on, even with his binoculars.

Images at that distance were mostly indistinct, but he could make out the ghostly forms of people moving around on the opposite bank. They seemed to be ducking and hiding. Duri moved closer and strained to see downstream, identifying a small bridge Mahmud would have to pass under. On the embankment below the bridge, Duri found what looked like three Humvees. He had to assume Mahmud was the intended target of this apparent ambush.

Duri immediately took action to protect his
investment. He moved quickly downstream toward the
bridge, stopping occasionally to inspect every detail of the
area. Ahead, an old wooden shack stood on the bank's
summit, about a hundred meters from the bridge. The
General had checked it out on his previous scouting
missions, but never understood its purpose. As best he
could figure, the rickety shelter had been a guard outpost
of some sort, and had long since been abandoned.

Duri entered through the door that faced away from
the river, then moved to the opposite wall, just a few steps
in. It, like the sidewalls, had a small window crusted with
dirt. Duri rubbed off enough gunk that he could observe
the Americans setting up the ambush, and soon realized
there were about a dozen soldiers ready to intercept
Mahmud on the opposite side of the river.

As Duri continued to watch the Americans, a major
problem presented itself. Six of them broke off from the
others and jogged up the embankment to the entrance of
the bridge. They intended to cross over. He had no choice.
Duri had to act fast to disrupt the two squads while
signaling Mahmud to abort.

Fortunately, the General had meticulously planned for
many contingencies. He unsheathed the hunting knife
strapped to his leg and crouched to his knees. After some
prying, the wooden planks loosened. Below the floor, Duri
found an RPG launcher that he had buried there months
earlier.

Duri quickly loaded the weapon and prepared to fire.
He grabbed a box of RPG's, then left the little shack. The
six soldiers had nearly made it half way across the river
before Duri reached the metal guardrail near the entrance

to the bridge. From his crouched position, he peeked across at the oncoming soldiers, who were jogging two-by-two. They had not seen him yet, but would be on top of him soon.

The General shouldered the launcher, stepped up to the concrete, and fired the first volley. The missile whizzed from the launcher in a cloud of white acrid smoke and landed well in front of the squad, exploding with a loud concussive pop. This had the desired effect. Some of the soldiers recoiled, while others fell to the ground in the chaos. Good, it would take a few moments for them to recover from the surprise attack, and that was exactly what he needed.

Duri had already sprinted across the road to the other corner of the bridge before the soldiers regrouped. He quickly dropped to one knee and reloaded for his next attack. The next round took off just as one of the soldiers was training Duri in his sights. But the concussion from the RPG jarred his grip on the rifle, preventing him from squeezing off a decent shot.

The squad decided to spread out and fall back, but Duri had already retreated. He headed southwest, angling away from the river. Minutes later, the Humvees came barreling across the bridge, loaded with soldiers wearing night vision goggles. Duri looked back from a tree line that he had just reached, knowing they could still see him. He would have to fight hard and smart to make it to the outskirts of the city of al Kut. But it would not matter. Mahmud had already escaped, heading upstream to the second rendezvous point.

* * *

Reid and Buzz heard the first explosion from their position downstream of the bridge. They had set up their sting operation on the east side of a ravine that cut deep into the soft ground and angled into the Tigris. The agents hid behind palm bushes nestled at the edge of the ravine's upper ridge, ready to intercept their targets. Now they wondered if they would get that chance.

The waters flowing in the river below backwashed into the small inlet, lapping at the earthen walls. The constant splashing produced enough noise to make getting an exact bead on the fighting difficult. But there was no mistaking where the action was after the second explosion.

Buzz pointed in the direction of a faint orange glow that nearly coincided with the sound. They quickly deduced that it had to come from the bridge a few hundred meters to the northeast. A few rounds of automatic rifle fire followed. Reid switched on a radio scanner, trying to pick up chatter, while Buzz moved to get a better look. He found a spot closer to the river and used a high-powered night vision scope to hone in on the bridge.

"Reid, I make out two Humvees high-tailing across that bridge heading southwest. Can't find what they're after."

Reid hit a button on the radio scanner, letting it strobe through all channels. "How far past the bridge can you see?"

"Can't really see anything. Why?" Buzz asked.

"The radio picked up communications between some soldiers. One unit is pursuing a small boat that kicked its engine on and took off upstream."

Buzz jogged back within earshot to listen to the chatter. It soon became evident that the Army had learned of this meeting and were now in the process of losing the General and Mahmud. The man in the boat had somehow disappeared, but the Humvees were still chasing the one with the RPG launcher.

Buzz gleaned as much information as he could about the pursuit from the scanner and guessed they could not be too far away. Then, another RPG impacted an area near and to the left of their position, confirming Buzz's estimate. He exchanged the scope for a radio, and prepared to join the pursuit.

"Where do you think you're going?" Reid asked, grabbing his arm.

"Thought I'd help those guys out. I've matched the frequencies on our radios, and I'll have the earpiece in if you need to contact me. If I don't answer, I'm listening, but can't respond," Buzz said.

"I'll contact Naseth. The shooting probably spooked his subject, but I'm sure they prepared for this. Maybe there's a secondary rendezvous point he'll lead us to," Reid said.

"Good, keep me informed."

As he stepped away, Reid called out, "Be careful!"

Buzz just smiled like a little boy about to get himself into trouble, then turned toward the chase.

Reid packed up the remaining equipment and started the half-mile hike to her vehicle. She had only a few minutes before Naseth would contact her via satellite phone at the scheduled time. She needed to be ready to roll as quickly as possible, but the sudden dilution of manpower concerned her immensely. Without Buzz, she and Naseth might have their hands full trying to corner the men they were hunting. And contacting the Army for help would not be an option.

Chapter Fifteen

General Duri crouched behind a low wall lining the main road leading into al Kut. The Humvees had just passed him. Looking up, he noticed that now they had help in their search. A Black Hawk helicopter made a pass above the cluster of buildings to his rear, but it too missed him. Duri waited for the Black Hawk to move on before he made his foray into the industrial sector of town. The buildings that the helicopter had just inspected were mostly empty warehouses sitting on the outskirts of the city. They had once been borrowed by the Iraqi military to store rations, so Duri knew their layout.

The General had also visited them on his recent scouting mission, hiding more weapons and ammunition inside the smaller brick building in the center of the complex. He carefully made his way to that warehouse, constantly checking the area for movement. By now, the soldiers had probably passed him by. Their chances of finding him were rapidly diminishing, but Duri knew better than to let down his guard.

Duri slinked across a vacant lot and found an opening in the fence at the building's perimeter. The surrounding darkness seemed tranquil; only the distant thumping of helicopter rotors faded in and out. Still, he searched the area with his binoculars out of an abundance of caution before proceeding to the entrance.

The door had remained locked since Duri was last here. He used a key to open it, and quickly scanned the dark interior for signs of trouble—there were none. He could detect nothing abnormal in the wide-open space, so he slipped inside, locking the door behind him. Duri tossed the bulky RPG launcher to the concrete floor and went in search of more important items. Food was at the top of the list.

Other than the warehouse floor, the building housed a small office at the rear. Duri opened the door to the cramped room, then climbed on top of a wooden crate. He removed a loose ceiling tile and found a box of supplies, including rations and a submachine gun with plenty of ammunition. He decided to take the weapon and leave the launcher behind to lighten his load.

As Duri stocked up, something clicked behind him. He whipped around, brandishing the newly-acquired weapon, but saw nothing. His instincts kicked in—there was something wrong. He had left the door open when he entered the office, but now it was closed. Someone had to be out there. He slowly made his way down from the crate and watched the open warehouse floor through a glass wall that surrounded the office. As he reached for the doorknob, Duri caught a glimpse of a human form reflected in the window. He flinched and spun, but a sharp blow to the head stopped him cold.

Buzz watched General Duri's limp body slide down the door and slump to the ground. He popped a glow stick, illuminating the office in green light. After kicking the gun away from the unconscious man, Buzz pulled out a deck of cards. He flipped through them and eventually found the one he wanted. The picture matched.

Buzz flicked the card onto the General's chest, then pulled out his radio. "Reid, come in."

"I read you, Buzz. Any luck?"

"Oh, not really."

"Damn!"

"What about you?"

"Naseth's subject was spooked by the gunfire at the bridge—just as we thought. He's camped out near the river."

"What's he waiting for?" Buzz asked.

"Naseth has been using a parabolic mike to monitor the suspect's communications. Apparently, he won't meet at the next rendezvous for three more hours. He's giving it time to die down, I guess," Reid said.

"So, what now?" Buzz asked.

"I'm heading back to base to bitch to Block about this ambush. You come back to the bridge and stay close in case Naseth calls with a change of plans."

"OK, but go easy on the big guy, will ya? He's very sensitive," Buzz gibed.

"If I end up shooting him, take over the investigation."

"Careful, I don't want to have to go to the stockade to visit you."

"Over and out, cowboy."

"Over and out."

Buzz bound his prisoner before throwing him over a shoulder. He figured Reid wouldn't mind if he disobeyed orders and met her back at the base with his surprise guest. Especially since he planned to thoroughly embarrass Colonel Block.

* * *

Reid stormed into the front door of the palace command center, startling several officers milling around the foyer. She brushed past them on her way to the computer room to confront Block. The two male officers

76

seemed more amused than offended, watching her stomp across the fine marble floor.

Reid turned the corner and found Block, the source of her anger, casually leaning back in a chair with his feet propped up next to a monitor. Block sipped coffee from a Styrofoam cup and stared at the oncoming thorn in his side.

"Agent Reid. Nice to see you made it back to the base in one piece. Did you have any luck out there tonight?" Block asked cordially.

She never slowed down or tried to answer. A swift leg sweep, followed by a forearm thrust, sent the oversized colonel backwards, over the top of his chair. He slammed hard onto the ground right between the shoulder blades, letting out a short, loud groan. Hot coffee splashed all over his chest.

"Shit, Reid. What the hell?" Block barked.

"Shut up, you moron! I don't know how you found out about the meeting, but your ambush just scared away our two suspects!"

Block looked away; he couldn't argue the point. He had monitored the raid's progress, and realized how badly it had fallen apart. He pulled himself to his feet and brushed off beads of hot liquid, trying hard to swallow his immense pride. Even though he outweighed her by at least a hundred and fifty pounds and stood over a foot taller, Block backed away.

"Agent Reid. This is a military operation. I take full responsibility for the failure in al Kut, but it was my mistake to make. You had no right to try and keep that information from the Army."

"See, that's what you're not getting," Reid shot back. "According to the President of the United States, this is my investigation. You're the one who's withholding information."

Block glanced at a video feed showing camera views from around the complex. An unscheduled helicopter landing had just taken place, and he watched as Buzz stepped out first. Reid turned to see what Block was looking at, then smiled when she saw several soldiers followed by Buzz carrying an unconscious prisoner.

Buzz strode confidently into the palace and met Block and Reid near the main entrance. He nodded and turned to his catch. "Agent Reid, Colonel Block, allow me to introduce my new buddy, General Shakir Amin al Duri."

The soldiers gently set the heavy man on the ground, then saluted the colonel. He returned the gesture and studied the General's face in amazement. Blood-soaked bandages covered some of his features, but it was him without a doubt. Buzz extended a hand, presenting Block the playing card with the General's name and face. The colonel took it and stared dumbfounded as Buzz walked toward the front door.

Reid stifled a laugh and followed him inside. "Good job, cowboy. I think he was thoroughly embarrassed."

Buzz slowed a little to let her catch up. Reid came close, wearing that same seductive look from earlier in the day. She placed a hand on his back as they walked inside.

Buzz liked the closeness. "You enjoyed that, didn't you?" he whispered.

The partners entered a short hallway that led to the back of the palace, and to their office. Reid turned and blocked his way. The softness in her eyes hinted at things to come, and he was quickly giving in. As she pressed against him, Buzz lifted her onto a step where they were now eye-to-eye. She was gazing at him longingly.

Although they had both agreed not to get involved, Buzz knew they were both too hot now to let it pass. Reid cradled her arms around Buzz's neck and kissed him long and hard. The two lost themselves in the moment, but were snapped back to reality by a noise in the main corridor. Buzz pulled away just before an officer rounded the corner, nearly colliding into them.

Buzz awkwardly let him pass, then exhaled in frustration. "OK, Agent Reid," Buzz said just loud enough for the officer to hear. "I'll meet you back at the office in five minutes to discuss those files. Don't be late."

The soldier shot them an odd look as he disappeared down the corridor. Reid looked up at him with a wry smile. "Better make it thirty seconds," she ordered, brushing her hand lightly across his chest.

Buzz stood in the hallway, watching Reid's hips swaying in those tight fatigues as she sauntered away toward the office. "Damn," he muttered. When he had cooled down enough to think again, he followed her.

It was clear that he would have to let Block start questioning the General. Besides, the colonel would have to wake him up first, and that could take some time—he smiled at the thought. When he got back to the office, he darted inside and locked the door behind him. Before he knew it, Reid was all over him. Yes, the interrogation would have to wait.

Chapter Sixteen

In the computer room, Block gathered files covering everything the U.S. military knew about General Duri, Hashimi, and Mahmud. Sedal entered and sat at his workstation, anxious to do some housekeeping he had put off for the previous two days. But Block had other plans for his right-hand man.

"Ah, Lieutenant, I'm glad you're here. I need your help in the observation room."

Sedal closed his eyes in frustration as the monitor lit up; but he listened to his orders nevertheless.

"First, I want to meet with the agents to discuss our strategy," Block said. "I'd like to be a little more cooperative this time. I think they've earned it."

Sedal had not arranged a system to contact the agents other than searching for them on foot. He had nearly walked out of the room before remembering one asset he had in place that could save him the exercise. "Colonel, does this mean you want me to shut down the PackBot surveillance?"

Block paused as Sedal tapped on his computer keys. "I said I want to be more cooperative, not naïve. I'm sure they'll continue to withhold information. They're the CIA, for Christ's sake."

Sedal chuckled. He knew it was true. With a few more clicks, the muted video feed from the PackBot appeared on screen. The lieutenant, slightly embarrassed, called out to Block who had nearly left the room. "Colonel, I don't think the agents will be joining us any time soon."

Block could not see the screen from his position, but Sedal's face and his tone of voice aroused his curiosity.

He circled the table and took in the images on the screen. "Well, Lieutenant, there goes any chance that you may have had of getting together with agent Reid."

Sedal shrugged off the verbal jab, as Block cracked a rare grin. The colonel suddenly realized he might have to take on the General alone and set out to prepare for the task. As Block headed for the door, Sedal closed the video feed and asked, "Do you want to hear the audio?"

Block responded without breaking stride. "Hell no! Shut it off and go wake up the General."

* * *

General Duri sat in the interrogation room, as straight and proud as he could, staring directly at the two-way mirror. Considering the pain he felt, it would be difficult to keep up the appearance and dignity befitting a general. He shifted the ice pack in his right hand and winced as the cold met fresh skin.

Opening and closing his jaw produced clicking sounds at the joint, but the muscles and tendons needed to be worked. Already, Duri knew it was dislocated at the temporal mandibular joint, and he would likely have to drink from a straw soon. He had endured this injury once before and dreaded the difficulty of the next few weeks.

The audience watching from the observation room included Block, Sedal, and now Hashimi, who entered the room cuffed and under guard. Block decided to take the good cop approach that Buzz had used so effectively with the prisoner. It had produced valuable intelligence, resulting in the General's capture.

Block nodded to the guard. "Go ahead and take those cuffs off." While the soldier followed orders, Sedal picked up a black leg brace with an attached transmitter and placed it on Hashimi's leg. Block offered Hashimi a clove cigarette, then presented a lit match. "There, that's a little better I would think. The leg brace will allow you to roam the grounds for a few hours a day—under guard of course. Just don't go too far, or it'll explode."

Hashimi thought he had seen that on American TV somewhere, and took the comment seriously. "How far is too far?"

Sedal alleviated his fears. "He's joking. We'll get paged by the tracking software if you go outside the base. If anything, we'll just track you down and shoot you."

Hashimi finally got the joke and laughed before turning to the General. His jovial smile turned smug as he gloated over the sorry state of his former superior officer. "I think he looks like camel shit. Good."

Block sidled up next to him. "I thought you'd enjoy seeing him like this. We caught him near the location you gave us."

Hashimi's smile widened. "He knows this?"

"No, not yet. He may not know what year it is right now. Buzz knocked him silly when he made the arrest."

Just then, Buzz slipped into the room, drawing Hashimi's attention. Block and Sedal stifled laughs and tried looking away.

"So, did I miss anything?" Buzz asked.

Sedal snorted. "Oh, I'm sure whatever you've been doing was far more exciting than this."

Block turned his back to hide a smirk, but Buzz caught on. They somehow knew about his encounter with Reid—but how could they? "Man, you guys need to grow up."

Block gave Buzz a friendly pat on the back. "Good job, by the way. I wish you hadn't hurt him so bad, though. That's my job." Buzz quickly recognized the new attitude of cooperation the Army had suddenly developed. He was dubious, but played along.

He shot Block a sideways glance, then turned and shook hands with Hashimi, who still seemed confused by the jovial atmosphere. But Hashimi enjoyed seeing his new friend getting the credit for Duri's capture. "You are the Lone Ranger, Buzz," Hashimi said.

The comparison to a childhood idol went over well. Buzz swelled with pride as he studied the beaten man in the next room. "Colonel, why don't you go in first. That way I can get a handle on your line of questioning."

"Good. Watch him and talk through my earpiece if you see anything unusual." Block grabbed his files and straightened his uniform before entering the room.

Upon noticing Block's rank, General Duri stood. Block made instant eye contact and nodded. "General, I am Colonel Warren Block. I am with the United States Army Intelligence unit here in Baghdad. I'm going to ask you some questions."

Duri grabbed the ice pack from the table and sat back down, staring almost dismissively at the mirror. "I am a general. Why do you not send a counterpart of equal rank? No offense to you, Colonel, but I feel I at least deserve this much respect." He spoke English even more smoothly than Hashimi, with an air of superiority in his voice.

Block stopped fiddling with the papers and stood tall, nearly at attention. "I apologize for the perceived disrespect for your rank, General. I know how it must feel to be placed in your position. I also apologize for the further insult at the manner in which you were captured."

Duri shifted his gaze back to the colonel. "I accept your apology, but I will not answer any questions from a soldier of lower rank."

"With all due respect, General, you don't have a choice in the matter. The man who captured you is not a soldier. He works for the CIA. You are being investigated for possible links to terrorists. You are being held under their rules, not military courtesies. And, you will be charged for war crimes for murdering your own men."

A long silence followed as Block once again searched through his files. Inside the observation room, Hashimi watched Duri's movements carefully. Buzz noticed a perplexed look on his face. "What's wrong?"

Hashimi furrowed his brow and glanced at the monitor displaying an extreme close-up picture of the prisoner's eyes. "I do not know my friend. Something is not right." Buzz trusted Hashimi's instincts and waited for him to figure it out.

Block found the paper he needed and skimmed the contents before his opening question. "First of all, do you know an Ibrahim Salih Khalifa al Hashimi?" He asked the question to help Sedal establish a baseline for monitoring the General's biometrics.

"Yes, he is my lieutenant."

Block noticed Duri's muddled expression. "You may have a concussion, General. Do you know what year it is?"

Duri scowled at the strange question. "Of course, 2003, April by your calendar."

"Good, just checking. Now, we know you were protecting another man on the river. Our troops lost contact with him. Where is he going next?"

Duri stared with the same dazed expression. "I do not know. It is out of my hands now."

"What is out of your hands? Why is this man so important?"

The aching prisoner turned back to the mirror. "Unlike my little pawn in there, I will not beg for a deal."

Buzz watched Hashimi's reaction slowly transform from puzzled to amused. "I guess we had it right, Hashimi. The General has been using you all along to mislead us."

"I think this is true. You will waste time with this man. He will only tell lies."

Everyone there had already figured as much. But secretly, the agents knew they might have another chance to catch a more important target. And this time, Block would not get the chance to intervene.

Chapter Seventeen

Agent Naseth settled into a comfortable position on the high ground of a steep creek embankment and closely watched his subject, the man he had borrowed water from at the Basrah shop. For cover, he used a large diameter pipe that ran west on the high ground along the small tributary, disappearing somewhere in the darkness. Below, the suspected terrorist descended into the shallow pools of the creek bed and waited for his contact.

The inlet fed into the Tigris River like the one Reid and Buzz had staked out earlier that night—though, here, the shallows covered a broader area with a wider mouth that could accommodate a small boat. Naseth concluded this had to be the right place, and the right time.

Somewhere across the ravine, Buzz and Reid monitored the creek bed and prepared to arrest the subject, and Mahmud when he arrived. They had all agreed on radio silence unless the situation warranted emergency contact. Each agent knew the plan, and now Naseth's job was to provide back-up and cut off any potential escape while his two partners made the arrests.

Naseth continued assessing the area until the low sputtering sound of an outboard motor rose from the direction of the Tigris. He shifted his attention to the tiny boat as it drifted into the shallow pool. The engine noise stopped abruptly and the lone pilot guided the craft with a wooden oar. Then, a faint blinking light signaled the waiting contact in code.

The call sign was answered, and the pilot brought the boat to rest on the mud flats near the steep embankment on Naseth's side of the creek. This scenario was not ideal, but the shallow water, combined with the creek's narrow width, posed only a minor obstacle for Buzz and Reid. Still, Naseth would have preferred the two men meet on the opposite side of the water.

The suspect waded into the shallows and grabbed the boat's bow. Mahmud stepped into the ankle deep water, and the two men exchanged greetings. Now Naseth could get a much better view of the flat-topped boat with its crates stacked across the stern. One detail immediately bothered him. All the crates were completely closed except one. Naseth saw an exposed rifle barrel sticking out of the open container. Luckily, it was out of reach.

As Naseth assessed the weaponry, the suspects stepped onto the bank and started a strange ritual, one that Naseth had never seen before. Mahmud took off all his clothes, except his skivvies. Then the other man grabbed something out of a burlap bag he had carried from Basrah. He flipped a switch on a battery-powered unit, and an eerie glow filled the darkness below. Naseth could not believe his eyes. Mahmud's skin lit up with writing on almost every square inch.

The light went out and Naseth switched back to his night vision binoculars. He watched Mahmud begin to dress, then jolt, as if he had been stung by a bee. The other suspect didn't notice until the painted man fell to the ground.

The suspect lurched forward and yanked Mahmud's limp body from the mud. Frantically, he looked around, but the pale moon provided too little light. Panicked, the suspect managed to plop the unconscious man onto the flat deck at the bow of the boat and grab the AK-47 from the open crate. His vulnerability became evident as he searched high and low for the attacker, then hid behind the flimsy fruit and vegetable crates.

Naseth quickly decided this qualified as an emergency situation and tried to warn Reid by radio. Unfortunately, she could not answer. Reid had moved in on the left side of the boat, trying to flank the gunman. But Buzz had shot the man with a dart before she could get into position.

Reid sloshed through the water about a hundred meters from the boat, drawing the suspect's attention. He responded by spraying the area with bursts of automatic fire. Bullets pelted the water around Reid, following her all the way to dry land. The suspect could no longer locate her without the aid of moving water, so he shielded himself and aimed between containers.

A loud clank from the front of the craft startled the suspect, causing him to jump into the open. He craned his neck for a better look at the source of the noise, and just then something exploded. The shockwave from a concussion grenade not only knocked Mahmud off the boat, it tossed the armed suspect up and backwards. He slammed into the water, but quickly staggered to his feet.

Buzz rushed in hard from behind, not even slowing to draw his weapon. He wanted the man alive. But the suspect had somehow held onto his gun. Out of the corner of the gunman's eye, he saw the blurry form of a man closing in fast. He whipped the AK-47 to his left and squeezed off a quick burst of bullets into the air before catching his balance. Buzz stopped short, reaching for his sidearm. Each man drew aim on the other. Buzz heard three shots, but they did not come from his adversary.

The suspect lost his grip on the rifle, dropping it harmlessly into the water. Naseth stood tall, lowering his pistol as the gunman fell sideways. He searched for Mahmud and found him face down in the water. He turned the unconscious man onto his back as Buzz fished the other suspect out of the water. Both worked furiously to save the men's lives, but only Naseth succeeded. He managed to clear the water from Mahmud's lungs and get him to breathe.

Buzz, on the other hand, had no such luck. He gave up and joined his partner on dry land. After checking the bank, Buzz found a fully-functional light unit like the broken one he had analyzed. Once they had secured the unconscious prisoner, Buzz searched the darkness, calling Reid's name. She responded, and Buzz found her sitting in the dirt, tying a tourniquet around her bloody right thigh.

"Don't worry, cowboy, it's just a flesh wound."

Buzz leaned in, worried, and helped her tighten the cloth. When he finished, she reached up and kissed him on the cheek as he lifted her off the ground. "You should get that looked at as soon as we get back."

Reid smiled, tightening her arms around him as he carried her toward the boat. "Are you going to carry me all the way back to base?"

"Hell no," Buzz said.

For a moment, his seriousness shocked her, but as he began to smile, she laughed and playfully tried to push free. "Hey, take it easy. Naseth just killed that gunman. It's the first time for him; he might be a little shaken."

"Watch him closely then, Reid said. "If he needs a psych consult, make him go, even if we have to send him back to the States."

Buzz agreed as they approached their partner. Naseth spoke calmly on the satellite phone to another agent in

Basrah about the provincial official who had visited the target house so often. He was all business, showing no signs of mental stress. That bothered Buzz. He would monitor Naseth very closely over the next few days.

* * *

Buzz desperately needed sleep, so he headed for CIA headquarters at the back of the palace. The sun had risen nearly an hour earlier, but time had little meaning to a man who had been awake for days. He found the room and shook the locked door. Inside, something moved, drawing his attention. Buzz rubbed his bleary eyes and peered through the small window at a surprising sight.

The PackBot that Sedal left him as a gift had obviously been used as a Trojan horse. Buzz watched as the camera at the end of the metal arm shifted while hovering over Reid's laptop. Another probe plugged itself into the computer's side and began hacking data. The robot did all of this while the remote sat idle on the desk where Buzz had left it.

"Basic model my ass," Buzz said under his breath, but loud enough for Reid to hear as she limped behind him.

"What are you talking about?"

Buzz turned away from the window and shushed her. "Hold on a second. Peek into the room—quietly. I know how Block found out about the meeting."

Reid leaned in and absorbed the unbelievable scene. "My God. I guess he's just playing nice. Got to hand it to the bastard; he's not just some dumb drill sergeant after all."

"No, he's not. So, what should we do about this?"

Reid hobbled away from the door and pondered her options. "Well, I don't know about you, but I'm too tired to come up with something right now."

"Me too. Let it finish, and we'll both get some rest for a couple of hours. Naseth should have the tattoos translated by then. I told one of the medics to check in on him and to let me know if he's acting strange. You'll have to take over the translation duties if he needs a break."

Reid grabbed Buzz's hand and lowered herself to a sitting position against the wall. He cringed at her obvious pain, then peeked into the room. After a few minutes, the PackBot disengaged and shut itself down. Buzz turned to inform Reid, but she had already drifted into dreamland. He carried her into the room, wishing they had more than the next few hours to rest.

Chapter Eighteen

General Duri studied his own reflection in the mirror from across the interrogation room table. He knew at least one person most likely watched him from the opposite side, but his obsessive urge to groom himself took over, though the shackles made this difficult. As long as he was alone, the mirror tortured him. Duri constantly patted his hair and straightened his U.S. Army issue jumpsuit, waiting anxiously for someone to come in and harass him again.

Duri's irritation grew to such a point that he felt the need to vocalize. "I need a trimmer! And I protest these humiliating prison clothes! I am a general, damn it!"

The door opened, as if on cue, and Buzz entered, gloating and carrying the light unit he had seized overnight. The distraction calmed Duri, and he immediately took on his usual smug persona. Buzz set the device on the table and walked back to the door. The General recognized the contraption, but merely sat back in his chair and grinned. Buzz motioned to the hallway outside the room and Mahmud appeared with a military escort.

The CIA's newest prisoner clearly had not expected to see the General, and paused briefly before the MP ushered him in and removed his cuffs. Mahmud locked eyes with Duri and showed his hatred for the man through a sinister gaze. Buzz wasted no time with small talk, interrupting the silent standoff by tugging on Mahmud's shirt. The prisoner obliged, ripping the tattered garment from his body and throwing it at the General. The sudden outburst caused Duri to flinch, which clearly hurt his battered head. Mahmud felt better and relaxed a bit.

Block studied the light unit with great interest from inside the observation room. The device was new to him, and the strange glow looked different than any light he had ever seen. Again, the agents had not properly briefed the colonel, but he decided to just roll with it. Block would learn its purpose soon enough.

After Naseth entered the interrogation room, Buzz motioned to the ceiling while addressing the mirror. "Kill the lights." A few seconds later, the room went dark, except for the area around the light unit.

Buzz picked up the contraption and scanned Mahmud's exposed skin, revealing the hidden writings. The tattoos both surprised and puzzled Block. Sedal, who had quietly manned the controls to this point, now gawked absentmindedly at the green glow. Then he snapped out of it, realizing he had forgotten to set the computer to digitally record the camera shots. Both soldiers began to understand the importance of the prisoner the CIA had captured.

Turning to Sedal, Block asked, "Why didn't we know about this backup meeting with Mahmud?"

"The PackBot can only give us what they put on the computer, or what it overhears in the office. The agents haven't been talking much inside. I don't blame them, frankly. The one time we did intercept info, we screwed up our ambush. The CIA is two for two without us."

Block knew that Sedal was right, but he stubbornly rejected the notion that the CIA could withhold information from the Army inside a theater of war. "I'm not just going to sit back and let the resources of the U.S.

military go to waste while they play keep away. I want you to continue hacking Reid's computer, and I want our own translators to verify Naseth's reports. I need a complete transcript of every tattoo as quickly as possible."

Buzz flipped off the light unit and tapped on the mirror. "Give me the lights."

Sedal hit the switch, then turned off the infrared on the cameras. Naseth whispered into Buzz's ear, then made some notes in his field report book. All the while, the General continued preening himself in the mirror.

Buzz moved between Duri and his reflection while Naseth, carrying the device, quickly ushered Mahmud out the door. "Well, General, that was creative. I'll give you that. But I guess you didn't plan on me now, did you? My fellow agent tells me the tattoos detail the locations of huge stockpiles of biological, chemical, and even nuclear weapons." This should have caused a reaction, but the General remained impassive.

Block issued another order to Sedal. "Leave the equipment the way it is and go get those translators. No excuses, this takes priority over anything they're working on."

Sedal tapped a few keys and rushed out.

Buzz tried to bait Duri again. "We know about the decoys in Agrah. Our agents are on their trail. You have nothing to bargain with. We're translating the writings as we speak, and our Army will find those weapons stockpiles soon enough. It's over for you, chief. That's it. So it's time for you to start begging for some leniency, maybe give up any more information you think we ought to have."

Duri stood while clapping his hands together loudly and slowly. "Congratulations, CIA agent. And to the U.S. military. I must commend you all on such outstanding work. You have truly outsmarted me and the lowly Iraqi Army." His sarcastic tone added to Buzz's trepidation. Block was not overwhelmingly confident either.

Duri shuffled around the table with his leg shackles clanging on the floor and extended a cuffed hand to Buzz. "Of course I am upset that my plan has been stopped, but I truly enjoyed watching the mighty U.S. Intelligence at work."

Buzz had heard enough sarcasm. He briskly rushed from the room with Duri laughing hysterically. Block joined the harried agent as they left to check Naseth's progress.

* * *

Buzz found Naseth busily typing as he carefully studied the fluorescent tattoos on Mahmud's back. Block followed him into the dark conference room located near the palace's grand foyer and stood momentarily in the doorway, allowing his eyes to adjust.

Naseth, clearly feeling the pressure of his role as interpreter, stopped typing and lashed out at the intruders. "Damn it! Shut the door! I can't read this with the light coming in!"

The men hastily moved into the room and closed the door as demanded. For several minutes, both of them acted like schoolchildren who had just been scolded by the teacher. Buzz particularly regretted upsetting his friend, considering Naseth's recent action in the field. Buzz could see the effects of the shooting had been exacerbated by the current assignment. The pressure had to be removed, so he finally approached his frenzied partner.

He placed a caring hand on Naseth's shoulder and spoke quietly. "Hey buddy, let's step outside. Take a little break."

Naseth stopped typing and turned. For a moment, he appeared to have stopped breathing, but finally exhaled with a low groan. It must have been a sigh of relief, because he left the room without protest, with Buzz on his heels.

Block let Naseth pass, then stepped in front of Buzz. "What's going on?"

Buzz let the door close and flipped on the light, revealing the occupants in the room, including two MP's, Mahmud, and Sedal. He turned his back on the unwanted company and spoke as softly as possible. "Agent Naseth had to kill a man during our raid. It's the first time he ever drew his gun in anger."

"I didn't know. I thought you were the shooter."

"I wish it was me. I got no problem droppin' thug terrorists, but not everyone's cut out for killing."

"And you think he's one of those."

"When I was a kid, my daddy took me and my little brother on a deer hunting trip to the Texas hill country. It was my brother's first time hunting, so when the first deer come along, he got the kill. Soon as he pulled the trigger, he froze. To this day, he hasn't touched any kind of firearm."

Block pursed his lips and huffed. "I understand. Maybe Naseth shouldn't be involved with this investigation; Sedal is supposed to be getting me some translators anyway. They'll finish this up. And we can use Reid too, if needed."

Buzz warily accepted. "That's fine, but either Reid or me will be back in here to review the transcript."

As Buzz left, Block turned to Sedal. "Where the hell are my translators?"

Sedal sprung to his feet, knocking over his bottled water. "Sorry sir. One will be here shortly, with a second translator to follow in twenty minutes or so."

As Block watched Sedal swab the spilled water from the table, he realized something that he had overlooked. "Lieutenant, I'm going to need your help a little later. Go get some sleep until I call for you."

Sedal responded with a half-hearted salute. When Sedal had left, Block decided to review the transcript and plan whatever action he could take with the available information. The prospect of staying up all night was nothing new. Block was an insomniac. Many attributed his nearly constant grumpiness to this fact. As Block went to work, Mahmud just watched in silence, his fate already sealed.

Chapter Nineteen

Reid crossed the well-manicured palatial grounds to a smaller building being used as a U.S. military infirmary. As she stepped into the foyer, she immediately noticed that, since her last visit, another wall had been removed to accommodate extra beds. But, for now, most of the space remained unused.

At the far end of the room, Naseth silently paced near a doctor and Buzz, who appeared to be deep in conversation with each other. When she noticed Naseth looking at her with a worried scowl, Reid limped in their direction. Naseth met her halfway. "Agent Reid, you gotta do something. They're talking about sedating me."

Reid took his hands and studied his face. "I know. That was my suggestion. I asked Buzz to keep an eye on you. He's concerned you're on edge."

"Of course I'm on edge. I haven't slept, and I just killed a man."

"That's exactly why you need rest."

Buzz approached with the doctor in tow. Reid looked to him for help. "Look buddy. We don't have to sedate you, but doc here says you need sleep."

The doctor agreed. "There's a room upstairs that's quiet. You can stay there for now."

Naseth gave in. "OK, but our next move is to go to Kurdistan to help agent Sumner, right?" Reid nodded. "OK, I'll get a few hours sleep, then Buzz and me will go together. He can prep for the trip while I'm resting."

Buzz shot Reid a worried look. "I don't know if that's such a good idea."

"Why? You don't trust me? I'm fine. If I don't get back on the horse now, I might as well quit the agency."

Reid bought into that argument. "I can't go with this leg. I would only slow you down. But we need to follow up on that lead. Those men killed a soldier, and I want them caught whether or not they're decoys." She paused, then added, "He's right, he needs to get back out there."

Buzz had reservations. "No offense, buddy. I just think I could go it alone. There's no need for a third agent out there. You should stay and rest."

"Sorry. If you go, I go," Naseth demanded, folding his arms defiantly.

Reid patted her partner on the back. "Looks like the Lone Ranger's taking Tonto with him."

Naseth slowly relaxed at the concession and headed for the stairs to take his doctor-ordered nap. "Don't forget to wake me up before you leave."

As he lumbered up to his room, Buzz led Reid back to the command center and updated her on the partial transcript of Mahmud's tattoos. For the time being, they were all business. But with every moment they spent together, separating business from pleasure was growing much tougher.

* * *

A regularly scheduled supply transfer provided an Army Chinook helicopter as transportation for Buzz and Naseth to an outpost south of Agrah. The Chinook's return trip would serve a more somber purpose—the transport of Darin Helton's body to Baghdad International Airport. Upon hearing that Buzz would join the search for

Helton's killers, agent Sumner requested a leave of
absence to accompany the casket on its long journey
home, back to Helton's family. Reid granted his request
without hesitation. The three agents would meet in the
field, and after a full briefing, Buzz and Naseth would take
over the hunt.

Buzz pondered the weight of his mission while
surveying the Kirkuk oil fields from the right side of the
helicopter. The view from above interested him, but his
partner seemed oblivious to their surroundings. Naseth
passed the time by checking and rechecking his sidearm.
Buzz could not help but wonder what psychological
damage had been done to his friend, and whether or not
bringing him along was a good idea.

After Naseth unloaded all the rounds from the
magazine for a third time, Buzz decided to snap him out of
his ritual. "How you doing there?"

Naseth heard him over the thumping blades and
answered coldly, "I'll be fine," while continuing his
obsessive behavior.

Buzz doubted his sincerity, but left him alone. After a
few minutes, the terrain began to change. Soon, the
Chinook rose substantially from the dusty valley below to
overcome the hills guarding the Kurdistan region of
Northern Iraq. The small rock outcrops quickly grew to
high plateaus elevated by charcoal grey cliff facings. Buzz
noticed low clouds hiding the mountains in the distance
and marveled at how quickly the topography and climate
had changed.

Naseth finally put his sidearm away when the Chinook
slowed dramatically and banked left. They were landing
just beyond a group of tents with one small wooden

structure at the camp's center. A contingent of soldiers greeted the agents warmly after touchdown, and one led them to the commander of this Special Forces unit. Lieutenant Colonel Robert Morgan, the same man who granted agent Sumner the use of one of his Rangers, now stood quietly near Helton's body at the back of the small medical tent. Naseth immediately related to Morgan's situation and could feel his anguish through the obvious signs. Morgan's body language betrayed him.

Buzz and Naseth stood at a distance as their escort quietly notified the commander he had visitors. Morgan snapped out of his daydream and gathered his composure before waving them over. Naseth stared absently at the covered body as Buzz approached. "Lieutenant Colonel Morgan, I'm Special Agent Buzz Foster and this…" He turned, but his partner had not followed his lead. "That man back there is my partner, Mark Naseth."

"Glad to meet you, Buzz. Sounds like a soldier's name."

"That's what my daddy thought. Gave me that nickname himself. Kept giving me buzz haircuts with the same shears they used on the sheep."

Morgan, obviously distracted, stared past him with a concerned look. "What's wrong with your partner there?"

Buzz spoke softly. "Naseth just had his first kill. I think the body is spooking him."

"Take my advice, Buzz. I've seen a lot of action. Don't take him out there in the field with you."

"I know, I know. He seems to think getting back into the field is the best medicine."

"In my experience, you're asking for trouble. There's nothing wrong with a little time off to process things."

Buzz was confused. "Doesn't sound like something an old soldier like you would say."

"There's a long tradition of armies trying to ignore the fact that warriors are just humans. It's never been smart, and the consequences have always been negative. I've seen it personally too many times."

"What about Helton here? What went wrong?"

The question prompted a deeper sadness in Morgan's eyes. "He had never engaged an enemy directly. I'm afraid I let him go into a situation he wasn't trained for."

Buzz ducked his head, then laid an open hand on Morgan's back. He felt the need to pay his respects and walked to the side of Helton's cot, then knelt down. As he started to pray, feet shuffled nearby. Buzz opened his eyes and realized Naseth and Morgan had joined him. For a few quiet minutes, the three men remained motionless with eyes closed. Once he had finished, Buzz rose to his feet and grabbed his sidearm. After checking the magazine, he declared, "OK, let's find the bastard who did this."

Chapter Twenty

Reid limped into the side door of a building she had not yet visited and surveyed the huge open space inside. A swarm of activity focused mainly around three rows of computer desks all facing the wall to her left. A dizzying array of television screens fed live images from soldiers' helmet cameras somewhere in the field. A few of the larger television sets displayed maps and other images relayed by the computers.

As she stepped onto the wooden floor, Reid guessed the building had been formerly used as a gymnasium. The openness of the venue, along with its proximity to Baghdad and the airport, created the perfect site to house the heart of the coalition operations in Iraq. And, of course, the Intelligence unit had a front row seat. Across the room, Colonel Block paced behind a group of computers manned by Sedal and several other soldiers.

Reid struggled through the maze of desks and equipment until she reached the bull-headed colonel. At first, he ignored her, while spouting orders and cussing the technology. Eventually, he calmed down enough to fill her in. "Agent Reid, welcome. I saw you come in and ordered a private to get a few extra chairs. Seems we have more computers than places to sit."

"That's fine. I'll just sit in Sedal's lap." She noticed the blood rushing to Sedal's face—the desired reaction. Then she turned back to Block. "So, I wasn't with the doctor very long. What caused you to move over here?"

"We've been in the process of setting up here since before you arrived. We finally got everything up and running. And our translators were able to isolate one location that could be storing a sizeable cache of chemical weapons. Colonel Holt over there is organizing a raid using a specially trained unit that can be at the site knocking on the door in minutes."

"How soon? I want the labs to be there."

"The site is just northeast of Baghdad, so it's an area that we've controlled since last week. Unfortunately, we weren't able to hold it as we moved into Baghdad, so we are reassessing the risks of sending soldiers in. We'll have to secure it before you do any testing."

"And your translators are continuing to work on Mahmud?"

Sedal answered while typing. "They're feeding us the unconfirmed transcript. I can pull it up any time."

"What about the confirmed transcripts?"

Again, Sedal had the answer. "It only has information pertaining to this site. I'm printing you a copy as we speak."

The private with the chair showed up just as Reid noticed her leg starting to ache badly. She gladly sat down. "Thank you, Private. Could you be a doll and find Sedal's printout and bring it to me?"

The soldier smiled. "Yes, ma'am."

Block frowned; apparently he didn't like his soldiers being addressed as if they were in a nightclub. "Agent Reid. I believe that pain medicine is making you a little loopy. Do you mind if I take your weapon for now?"

Reid straightened as she rolled to the left, exposing her sidearm. "Yes, I'm sorry. I should have known better."

Block reached down and removed the pistol. "Not a problem. This kind of thing happens. I'm just trying to be safe."

The private, who didn't seem old enough to be in the Army, returned with the transcript. This time Reid forced herself to address the private more professionally. "Thank you, Private."

As she flipped through the pages, she did her best to focus on the report, but it was a dry read and the descriptions made no sense. She was rubbing her temples when a voice startled her from behind.

"That shows where something is, uh. You can see the location is compared to other buildings, ten kilometers west of a mosque."

Reid shook off the cobwebs, looked up, then grabbed Hashimi's hand. "Good to see you're still helping us. You enjoying your little bit of freedom?"

"Yes, I look at the river for part of the day, not a concrete wall. Very nice."

"So, these names are holy sites?"

Hashimi pointed to several names on the paper. "Yes, most of these, yes. They are like uh…"

"Landmarks?"

"Yes, I think this is it."

Block slapped Hashimi hard on the back, causing a sharp pain. It was meant to be a friendly pat. "Once again, our friend Hashimi has come through. He even pointed out the location on a map for us. I'm thinking about taking off the ankle brace," Block said.

Reid tried hard to focus as she rummaged through her bag. "No offense to his obvious expertise on the country, but the CIA has analysts that could be confirming this information."

Once again, Block had been caught withholding information. Hashimi noticed the comment had changed Block's mood, and he knew by now to stay out of the way. He backed up, carefully leaving plenty of room for the giant. "Agent Reid, I know you think the DOD is just a bunch of clods, but I assure you the Army has access to plenty of our own analysts," Block insisted. "Holt wouldn't launch a raid without me confirming the intelligence."

Reid managed to open her laptop and switch it on. "All the same, it doesn't hurt to use every available resource to verify the information. Plug me into the network and I'll contact Langley. I want CIA analysts to get those transcripts just as fast as you get them. We won't make a move until they give a confirmation."

Sedal heard the request and stopped working. He looked to Block for direction and waited anxiously. The colonel reluctantly nodded his approval, sending Sedal back into action.

Hashimi nervously said, "I can tell you this is the place. I cannot say if you will find anything there, but this is what the markings says."

Reid had stopped listening and Sedal continued working on connecting her computer. Block gave up on the conversation altogether and walked over to update Holt. The tenuous relationship between the CIA and Army Intelligence had taken another downturn, but it seemed to Reid that both agencies had to remain determined to avoid a potential nightmare. They would have to somehow find a way to put aside their territorial issues and work together.

* * *

Naseth took on a familiar surveillance role, blending in with the local population while monitoring his subject's movements. Only this time, the subject was on his side, at least as far as he could tell. The man paced and smoked in front of what looked like an abandoned house matching the coordinates they had agreed upon in their earlier communication. He had expertly concealed his Caucasian features and moved liked the locals, but it could only be agent Sumner. Naseth had to admit, he was impressed by Sumner's mastery of the spy trade.

Sumner crushed out the cigarette and stepped inside. The house stood at the northern edge of town, overlooking farmland, so there were few people to cause concern. Still, the CIA always took extra precautions. After a few minutes, Buzz emerged from behind a nearby shed and took a slow, varied course to the house. Eventually, he reached the open door and slipped inside.

Sumner, waiting inside, greeted him with a handshake and a bottle of water. "Buzz? I'm Andrew Sumner. Glad to finally meet you. You're legend is growing in the agency."

Buzz smiled humbly. "Appreciate it."

"Sit down at the table. Look over these photos. Those are your men."

Buzz burned the faces into his memory. "What's your last lead on them?"

"They have used a short list of aliases. That second group of names is just what the locals call them here in Agrah. But Reid has identified them as Ayad Ammash Hasan and Rashid Yasin. Ayad, the older man, is a known associate of General Duri, but we've got no leads on the younger one."

"You think they're still here?"

"Well, if they're not, they couldn't have gone far. Ayad lost pints of blood. They had to stay together to get medical attention."

"Pretty hard out here."

"Almost impossible. We disrupted their plans, that's for sure. Rashid is the important one, but without the older guy, I don't think he would know what to do or where to go next."

"Sounds like the same set-up with the General. Have you seen either of these men carrying anything around like a portable light unit?"

"Not really. They abandoned their original hideout and I found nothing significant there. But they've carried bags around with them. Depending on how big this light unit is, they could've had it with them."

Buzz studied the list of names. "I'll have to show these to Naseth. Why don't you share with Reid. Tell her to run them past Hashimi. See if he recognizes any of them."

"OK. Also, I know the two men linked back up after the gunfight. Found a witness who saw them together."

"What about the local doctor?"

"Ah, that's where I left off. I drew a map, but haven't been there yet. He's sort of a doctor. Works on the livestock too."

"Reminds me of home," Buzz mused. "Was he easy to find?"

"Oh yeah."

"Then our men must have gone to him for help. If not, the old man is dead."

The agents stood almost simultaneously, then shook hands once more. "Good luck, Buzz," said Sumner.

"You too. You've got a tough trip ahead. I've got the easy part here."

Sumner wrapped his face and headed out the door. Buzz had his own plateful of problems. But, for now, he wanted food. He signaled to his partner and started rummaging through the supplies Sumner had left behind. Fortunately, Sumner was a man after Buzz's own heart. One burlap bag contained nothing but junk food, including half-melted candy bars. He dug in, knowing he would need the energy boost later.

Chapter Twenty-One

Block returned to his desk after conferring with Colonel Holt. Slowly, the noise level in the room began to drop as all the television screens displayed a single video feed from a PackBot camera. The giant speakers near the wall squeaked, followed by the voice of a soldier in the field.

"Colonel Holt, robot's ready to roll!"

Holt, standing only meters away at the center of the computer consoles, answered over the com link. "OK Corporal, send it in."

"Yes, sir."

The image on the screens shook as the machine moved across the gravelly ground toward a large building that resembled an old warehouse. Reid stared and listened in disbelief before pulling herself up on wobbly legs. After a few shaky moments, she painfully limped over to the console.

"Block! What's going on here? I haven't given you any confirmation on this site yet!"

Every soldier in the room turned and stared. Block cowered. "Let's talk about this later."

"It'll be too late by then! Do I have to knock you on your ass again to get this to stop?"

Colonel Holt rushed over to run interference. "You two settle this later. I'm going on Block's recommendations; it's too late to call this off now. Given that we're already in place, it can't hurt to go in and look around."

Holt did not wait for a response. He briskly walked back to his console and donned a headset. Reid found her seat and angrily plopped back into it. She could do nothing now but watch and hope for the best.

The PackBot reached a door on the side of the warehouse and stopped. The camera tilted upward and focused on the doorknob. Then a metal arm appeared on the left of the screen and extended to the knob.

A spinning saw blade at the end of the extension smoothly cut out a square piece of the door around the knob. The chunk of metal fell inside the building while the blade slowed to a stop. Not being anchored to the doorframe, the door naturally swung outward. The PackBot backed away to accommodate, and quickly launched an object into the building.

Upon impact, the PackBot's grenade exploded in a cloud of smoke. Seconds later, a stream of soldiers rushed into the building as the corporal screamed assault orders. Block proudly watched the precision operation, then turned to Sedal. "I love those damn robots!"

After a few minutes, the corporal spoke directly to Holt. "Colonel Holt, it's empty, sir. Not even a scrap of wood in sight."

"Damn it! Are you sure there's nowhere else to hide anything?"

"Positive, sir."

"OK. Double check it and pull out." Holt ripped off his headset and shouted at the men sitting near him. "Switch me over to the second site."

Reid's jaw dropped as the screens cut to another image, obviously originating from a different PackBot camera. The unit commander, Sergeant Jack Ward, started providing a play-by-play description of the action in the field. Alarmed, Reid shuffled through the papers and could find only unconfirmed transcripts. "You're not even waiting for the translators to confirm these?"

Block appeared concerned, but remained silently optimistic. The second team sent their PackBot rolling into action toward an abandoned warehouse. The second raid started much like the first. The remote-controlled machine stopped at a large wooden door and began cutting around the doorknob. But this time the operator had less than full command of the controls. The jerky movements made the images on screen jump around in a dizzying display.

As the saw blade extended, then cut, it skipped out of its groove several times. On its final pass, the blade slipped upward and skimmed past the metal knob, barely avoiding contact. Then, on its way back down, the blade tapped the knob ever so slightly.

Instantly, the screens turned static as the speakers bellowed. A deafening noise reverberated off the gymnasium walls, forcing everyone to reel and cover their ears. They had lost visual, but Sergeant Ward's audio continued relaying warbled sounds. As the thunder faded, the commander's cussing began, and continued even as Holt tried to interrupt.

Eventually he broke through the chaos. "Commander, this is Colonel Holt! What happened?"

"Sorry, sir, all hell just broke loose! The building exploded! We're pulling back and forming a perimeter!"

"The whole thing blew up?"

"Affirmative! We have wounded, sir! Need a medical evac for multiple personnel!"

"Affirmative. We'll send 'em out. I want an update on your situation ASAP!"

"Yes, sir!"

The audio disconnected and Holt angrily slapped his headset on the console. He looked around for a moment, then zeroed in on Block. In a sudden surge, Holt bounded across the room and careened into the bigger man. The ensuing melee resembled two bulls fighting for control of the herd. Half the roomful of soldiers entered the fray before the fight finally ended.

Reid managed to avoid the chaos, as well as further injury. After surveying the damage, she questioned the wisdom of having attacked Block earlier. Good thing for her he had decided to keep his cool, but she didn't want to confront him again. She concluded that the best course of action right now was to approach Holt instead, who was carefully tending his wounds.

"Look, that's not going to do any good. It was your decision to refuse the CIA's help. And how was anyone supposed to know the building would be rigged, anyway?"

She had Holt's attention. He knew he had acted too quickly, but refused to readily accept full responsibility. "I depend on Block for good intelligence and he just sent my men into a trap."

"No, Colonel. You sent them there, and you had a chance to avoid it. Let me explain a little more clearly why I'm here. The fact is, I've been inside Iraq running an intelligence gathering operation for more than a year before you ever set foot here. We have agents deep undercover in both the areas your men just went into. These agents have been reporting Iraqi troop movements and activities to me daily. Let's just say we didn't trust the weapons inspectors to keep track of everything."

Holt let this sink in for a moment. "Does Block know about this?"

"No, but the President does. That's why he sent me to assist Army Intelligence. Much of the planning that went into this invasion came to CENTCOM from me and my agents. Problem is, there's been a disconnect with me trying to work along side Block instead of filtering everything through Langley and CENTCOM. It's sort of wrecked the whole order of things. We need to work out how to share information."

Reid noticed Holt stiffen up. Block had slowly come up behind her as she lectured Holt. Holt stood tall and extended a hand to his old friend, swallowing his pride. "Warren, I apologize. That was uncalled for."

After a long moment, Block laughed and clasped his hand. "Hey, after all the messes you've helped me clean up, I can let this one go. Truth is, I put you in a bad spot. Got ahead of myself."

"I guess this is a learning experience," Holt said. "Looks like Mahmud is a decoy and you've got some work left to do. The real target is still out there somewhere."

"Mahmud has a pretty high profile protector to be a decoy. But you're right. I've got lots of work."

Block started to gather his papers, but Holt had one last suggestion. "Make your life a lot easier and listen to agent Reid. She has something to tell you that might convince you to cooperate with her a little more."

Block looked at Reid. He seemed a little confused. She handed him a briefcase, then helped him collect his papers. "He's right, Colonel. It's time we talked about restructuring our working relationship, for the good of the mission. We've let things get too out of hand."

Activities in the gymnasium slowly returned to normal. Reid hobbled out of the building while enlightening Block on her covert activities over the past year. He wished she had told him all of this much sooner, but realized his own arrogance may have prevented her from sharing. Both agreed it was time for Block to get more aggressive with Duri. The General had clearly masterminded this plot and he would have to answer for concealing information from the U.S. military. Block would enjoy their next meeting.

Chapter Twenty-Two

Buzz ducked behind a small rusted barn, leaving Naseth to watch the farmhouse alone. When he was out of sight, Buzz noticed a light blinking on the satellite phone. Upon answering the call, the sound of Reid's voice buoyed his spirits. But Reid's news soon put a damper on the conversation.

"Hi, cowboy. Good time?"

"If you're calling to bring me back in, then no, it's not a good time."

"Not even if I called you back on a personal matter?"

"Hmm. I might reconsider. But somehow I think you have other issues on your mind."

"All right, back to business, as usual. Looks like your assignment just took on a higher level of importance. Military units raided two sites based on Mahmud's tattoos. First one was empty. Second building was rigged. The explosion wounded three soldiers and killed one. Wiped out the buildings surrounding it, too."

"Shit! Any WMDs?"

"Mobile units didn't find any traces yet and they don't think they will. Air samples didn't indicate anything either."

Buzz leaned forward in his squatting position enough to confirm that Naseth was still there, raking hay into neat piles. "There's no telling how many decoys are out here. Surprises me, though, that General Duri risked being caught to protect a decoy."

"We've thought about that. Block is getting ready for an aggressive interrogation soon, but we won't learn anything new. The General won't cave. It's not part of his profile. Putting himself as the protector of a decoy may have been the smartest plan. Look at the time and resources we are spending on this."

"So he really was using Hashimi all along. He led us right to the General, then to Mahmud. I would think Duri would be smarter than to leak such important details unless he meant to."

"Maybe I need to interview Hashimi again. See if there are any clues to this theory. Maybe in hindsight it'll seem a little more obvious that Duri was dropping these bits of information on purpose."

"Good plan. Hold on."

Buzz covered the phone to listen to Naseth, who had stopped raking and left his surveillance post to report some important news. "Buzz, it looks like he's in there."

"Good. Head that way. I'll sweep the area and come around the back side of the house."

Naseth nodded and started his slow walk to the farmhouse, while Buzz wrapped up his call. "Reid, we're about to question the village doctor. He probably treated our injured suspect."

"Stay safe and report back soon."

"Don't you start worrying about me, now."

"I'm more worried about Naseth. Keep a close eye on him."

"I will. Bye."

"Over and out."

Naseth casually checked his back several times before Buzz appeared at the corner of the barn. He felt safer now, but kept a wary eye to his front. The only movement he detected near the house was a bunch of chickens milling about the yard. As he approached the small well-maintained house, muffled noises filtered through the screened windows. But there were no voices, only the clanging of metal on metal and shuffling.

Naseth angled in toward the right side of the house and casually glanced into a low window. The inside of the house was a large space separated by a wall down the center. He could see the kitchen at the opposite corner and a small living area up front, but no people. Next he moved to the screen door, where he had seen a man walk into the house minutes earlier. Naseth stayed close to the wall and leaned his head into the doorway. For a moment, he saw nothing. Then a man fitting Simi's description stepped from a room at the back of the house. The doctor, a hunched old hermit with a wildly unkempt beard, held up a hand and muttered something unintelligible.

Naseth assumed this was an invitation to enter and stepped inside without resistance. Speaking in Arabic, Naseth tested the waters. "Dr. Simi? Are you alone?"

Simi waddled away from the door and waved an arm, inviting him to follow. Naseth understood him better now. "Yes, young American friend. See for yourself."

Naseth was a little surprised by the fact that the old hermit had made him so easily, and flung away his long shirttails, revealing his sidearm. "How do you know I am an American?"

"Simple. This is a small village. We know our neighbors. We know everything that happens here. You are with another, outside somewhere I should think. Please, check. The men you are looking for are no longer here."

Naseth came closer and stood in front of the old man while scanning the room. "Could you step in there ahead of me?"

"Yes," the doctor said, and led the way.

After scouring the room, and then the rest of the house, Naseth began to relax when he found things to be in order. "I apologize for coming into your home this way."

"It is not a concern," the doctor said.

"Have you offered medical help to this man?"

Simi examined a photo. "Yes, he was hurt badly, but he will live."

"No offense Doctor, but not if I find him. He killed an American soldier."

Naseth watched his reaction, but Simi just turned and walked into the kitchen. "You need to go quickly. This man and his young friend were here only minutes before you came."

The realization that the two suspects had escaped detection worried Naseth and he grew more alert. "But we watched your house before I came in."

Simi stopped pouring water. "Were you by the barn? Then you could not see them. My patients stay in the shack behind my house. I was telling them he needs to stay and rest, but they did not listen. So I came back here."

Naseth rushed through the hall to the back door. "Why were you so calm? You should have said something!"

"And have a shootout in my home? I am old, but not a fool."

"Did they say where they were going next?"

"Yes, to Mosul. Unless they stole my car, you should catch them quickly."

Naseth stood at the open back door with his weapon drawn. The doctor joined him.

"Dr. Simi, did they have weapons?"

"I did not see weapons, but they have a bag."

Naseth stepped into the yard and studied the shack standing about fifty yards behind the house next to a palm grove. Through the wide palm leaves, he found the carport on the right side of the shack. He moved left to get a better view while Simi stayed at the doorway.

"Is that a carport?"

"Yes, you see my car?"

"No, it's empty."

The old doctor moved the fastest Naseth had seen him move. He looked like his best friend had died. "My car!"

Naseth ignored him and approached the carport. Before he could investigate, an engine roared to life on the opposite side of the tiny building. Then, gunfire. First, from the direction of the engine noise, then from a greater distance away. After a few more rounds, the car lurched forward.

The suspects were only a few yards away when Naseth reached the corner of the building. He pulled up into a firing position and had the driver's head in his sights. As the shots continued, Naseth froze. The car lurched forward and accelerated across a gravel road leading into the village.

Ahead, Buzz jumped into the car's path and unloaded his pistol, shattering the windshield but failing to stop the vehicle's progress. At the last possible moment, he rolled out of harm's way just as the car sped past. Buzz just stared back at Naseth, then thrust his arms up in a gesture of frustration.

Chapter Twenty-Three

General Duri did his best to walk with dignity as two MP's led him to a familiar room. He sat in the usual chair directly across from the two-way mirror, and immediately started grooming himself. The guards left him to his self-inflicted torture.

Block watched him anonymously with a hollow stare and folded arms from the other side of the mirror. Reid walked in with Hashimi in tow, but the tiny room remained quiet for several minutes, neither she nor Block willing to say a word. Finally, Reid decided to break the awkward silence. "You're showing remarkable restraint, Colonel. I thought you'd be in there working on him already."

"That might make me feel better, but it wouldn't accomplish anything by itself. I'm sure Hashimi would agree with that."

Hashimi had ignored the conversation until his name was mentioned. "Like I say. The General would never tell a thing. You may cut off both arms and still he never would talk."

Block sighed and reached for his files while Hashimi continued to study Duri. The colonel shuffled the papers for the hundredth time, then seemed to brighten with an idea. "Agent Reid. Has Buzz sent you any photos of our suspects in Kurdistan?"

"Yes. I showed them to Hashimi and had Langley run them through our databases. Nothing came of it. I also just handed them off to Sedal before coming here."

"Good. And there's nothing new on the search?"

"I'm waiting for a call. They were about to question the village doctor last I heard."

Sedal hurried into the room and sat at the computer without acknowledging anyone. Block waited, then, in his customary tactful way, slapped him lightly across his back. "Well, Lieutenant?"

"Oh, sorry. They're coming right now."

Reid interrupted. "Who's coming?"

The door to the interrogation room opened and several men entered. One of them carried the light unit Buzz had seized. Block turned on the microphone and spoke to Duri. "General, remove your shirt."

Duri shot straight up out of his chair in disgust. "I will do no such thing! This is an outrage!"

"We don't need to keep you awake for this," Block warned.

Another man, this time a doctor, entered the room holding a syringe with a large nasty looking needle. The sight seemed to make Duri reconsider, electing instead the more dignified method. As soon as his shirts were off, the room went dark. An MP scanned Duri's body with the special light, but contrary to their expectations, his skin contained no hidden messages.

Block ordered the men out of the room. A tense silence once more descended on the observation room. Duri sat, then resumed his routine, while Hashimi watched him closely. "Colonel, I think I know what is missing."

"Really? Would you be so kind as to tell me what that is?" Block stepped closer, anxiously awaiting anything that might break the stalemate.

Hashimi paused, still observing Duri closely. Something seemed wrong; something that had been bugging him all along. "That man is not General Duri!"

Sedal scoffed at the notion, then quickly displayed a file photo on one of the monitors. "Sure looks like him. What makes you think it's not?"

Hashimi studied the picture. "The General does a funny thing if he is nervous. He always pulls on his face hair."

"You mean his mustache?" Reid asked.

"Yes, this is right. He does this always. That man did not do this, even one time."

"He's been injured. Maybe he's just a little out of it."

"I tell you he is not Duri. Look, you see."

The observers scrutinized the man on the other side of the glass for a few tense minutes.

Sedal gave in first. "I'm going to use facial recognition software to run a comparison with Duri's photo in his file. It'll depend on the quality of that photo, of course, but I should be able to get a probability on subtle facial features." He glanced up at Block. "I'll have to use the software on my computer in the other room."

Hashimi offered one last bit of information. "Agent Reid, I tell you, the man who escaped in the tunnel is the real General Duri. From there, I do not know."

Block mumbled something to Sedal that spurred him to leave the room in haste. Reid abhorred the secrecy and refused to be left out of Block's plans. "What now?"

"A little surprise," Block replied. "You'll want to watch. I think this is where I start to lose my patience."

Moments later, Block stepped into the interrogation room and interrupted Duri's grooming. Both men eyed each other suspiciously, but exchanged no words until Sedal entered. He brought the same doctor who had been ready to administer the shot before, but Block had a different purpose in mind for him now. The doctor set a plastic tub on the table next to Duri and prepared another syringe, with a larger needle this time. Duri watched intently.

"I know what you're thinking, General," Block bellowed, interrupting Duri's icy concentration. "You're a weapons expert and a cold-blooded killer. What's to stop you from taking that needle and sticking it in my jugular?" Duri looked away from the doctor. From his history, it was likely that Duri was formulating some kind of plan, but Block's words seemed to dispel any plot the General might have been toying with. "Just remember something, General. Sedal here may not look like much, but he's the sharpest shot you're likely to ever see. He'd put a bullet in your skull before I could even form a fist to defend myself against you."

The General studied the mousy, bespectacled lieutenant who just glared back. "So why is this man standing by me with a big needle?"

Block spoke while Duri and Sedal continued to engage in a staring contest. "Just have to take some of your blood. It's required Red Cross crap—something about the Geneva Convention. These days an army can't go anywhere without lawyers and reporters tagging along— part of life now. It's better to just get it over with."

Duri broke eye contact and rolled up his left sleeve, offering up a vein. The doctor proceeded to fill the syringe, then quickly packed his kit.

"Are you sure that's enough for your DNA analysis?" Duri asked.

The doctor froze, confused. The colonel waved him on and sent Sedal back to the observation room. "Like I said, General. Just Red Cross requirements. They wanted to check your health personally, but they settled for a blood sample. They have a representative watching from the observation room."

"I know when people lie," Duri said. "They explain too much. You would do better to make your lies simple."

"Is that so?" Block said incredulously. "This coming from a man who has organized such an elaborate plan with invisible tattoos and multiple decoys to throw off the U.S. military."

"I see you admire my work."

Block ambled over and leaned against the table next to Duri. The General ignored the rehearsed intimidation and started grooming himself in the mirror again.

"You know, General, I notice you have this routine of fixing your appearance all the time. Sort of looks like an uncomfortable habit. You straighten your shirt, pat your hair. Every once in a while, you tug on your mustache." This got Duri's attention. "Now, from what I've been told, you almost always tug on that mustache. Even when there's no mirror around. Strange how you would suddenly act differently. I would think you'd be even more nervous under the circumstances. Make you want to tug the shit out of that thing. But you seem much calmer than the man that's been described to me."

"You believe the lies of a fool."

"Maybe that's just it. You said you can tell a liar when his story is too complex. But this is too simple to be a lie.

125

The General always pulls on his mustache. That's pretty simple."

"Hashimi has learned well from me," Duri sneered.

Block, now standing behind Duri's chair, lost his patience. With a sharp downward blow, he punched Duri hard in the side, cracking several of his ribs with a sickening snap. The General lurched forward, grabbing his side and leaning on the table like a rag doll. A few minutes passed before Duri fully caught his breath, and Block enjoyed every gasping moment.

"Hashimi did learn well from you. He learned exactly what you wanted him to know, then you set him up to be captured by us. You fed him the parts of the plan that would lead us to the decoys. Or, I should say, the real General Duri used Hashimi as his pawn. You're just an actor. A pretty damn good one, I'll give you that. But you're here to keep us busy while the real General is out there making sure the plan goes off."

The broken soldier held his busted ribs and sat up against the walnut paneling. "When my blood shows you it is me, you will feel sorry you did this."

Block nonchalantly responded as he headed for the door. "No, not really. I don't care who you are. I just want you to confess and tell me where the real target is. No decoys this time. I'll give you a few minutes to think about it and then I'm sending in some specialists. These guys treat torture as an art form. I can't wait to see them work one of their masterpieces on you."

"I wonder what the Red Cross and the lawyers think of this."

Block left Duri on the floor to do some thinking. Secretly, he hoped the man really was an actor. Torturing a general could bring high profile attention and heavy consequences. But the stakes had become too high to play by the rules.

Chapter Twenty-Four

A Little Bird helicopter patrolling the main road to the
east of Mosul slowed to a near hover and banked left. The
veteran pilot, Lieutenant Russell Jackson, had been
ordered by his commanding officer, Lieutenant Colonel
Morgan, to continue the search for a small car with a dirty
brown body and splotchy, sky blue roof. The two men
inside were suspects being hunted by the CIA and Army
Intelligence. So far they had managed to evade the Special
Forces squads Morgan had hurriedly assembled to capture
them. But Buzz had suggested to Morgan that they would
head for Mosul to rendezvous with suspected foreign
terrorists known to be pouring into Iraq.

Jackson would like nothing more than to capture or
kill men fitting this profile, so when he spotted a car on
the road below the chopper matching the description from
Intelligence, he immediately looped around to get a better
look. His copilot, Specialist Jon Whitely, read off the plate
numbers from a notepad and used binoculars to examine
the suspect car's plate. "Lieutenant, drop down a little if
you can."

"OK, but I want to stay out of his mirrors."

The helicopter slowly descended, and soon Whitely
had confirmation. "That's it. The plates match."

"Get Morgan on the radio."

Whitely worked rapidly through several radio
operators while Jackson followed at a seemingly safe
altitude and distance. In minutes, Morgan's gruff voice
boomed into their headsets. "All right, boys. Whatcha got
for me?"

Whitely adjusted his volume down and updated Morgan. "We got a car matching the description of those missing suspects and the plates match too. Heading due west into Mosul. Couple of miles out from the main section of the city."

"Have you passed any sizeable buildings, any landmarks?"

"No sir, but at this rate we're talking only a few minutes before we're into the urban population. Can't fire there."

"OK, hold for a moment. We're checking for ground units in the area. The Marines may have elements close enough to intercept."

"Affirmative, sir. Will hold."

Jackson checked his gauges and turned his radio off. "Whitely, he's speeding up."

"I can tell. Look there, in the passenger window."

An arm holding some object extended out the car window, followed by the head and torso of one of the suspects.

"Is that a gun?" both men asked simultaneously. From this distance, it was hard to tell for sure. Although Whitely knew they would not be able to see or hear gunshots, he was pretty sure that the suspects were now shooting at their helicopter.

Jackson casually moved out of the line of fire and the suspect disappeared inside the car. "They spotted us, but they're obviously not heavily armed."

Whitely tried to reach Morgan again. "Commander, we're being fired upon and the car sped up."

"Received," barked Morgan. "Ground units won't get there in time. Take the shot if you have it. But try to disable the car without killing them if you can."

"Affirmative, Commander. Going in for a strafing run," Jackson interjected. He straightened up in his seat and dropped the copter toward the ground.

The helicopter descended at a sharp angle of attack, closing in fast on the underpowered car. Jackson wanted to intercept the suspects before they reached a cluster of three buildings at the eastern perimeter of the city. Whitely pointed out vehicular movements just off the main road, beyond the two larger buildings on the right, but Jackson focused on the target. If he stuck to the center of the road, he felt civilian casualties could be avoided. But as the Little Bird leveled off into firing position, the possibility of collateral damage seemed imminent.

Jackson held the nose of the helicopter on a straight line down the center of the road. Then the two 7.62 inch mini guns exploded with a flurry of bullets, carving parallel lines across the concrete surface. The bullet trails zeroed in on the car's trunk and found their mark as the car drew even with the cluster of buildings. The back window shattered and the young driver made a severe right turn. The car slid sideways across the dusty ground, just missing the corner of the first building. The driver overcompensated and lost control. Seconds later, the car careened into a moving truck.

The helicopter abruptly slowed and spun in an about face. Ahead, dust clouds concealed most of the ground movement, but the rooftops of all three buildings swarmed with frantic activity. The pilots quickly realized the men were actually heavily-armed militants, not civilians. The suspects had reached the rendezvous point Buzz had warned Morgan about.

The mini guns opened up again, this time targeting the two buildings on the north side of the road. The overwhelming barrage sent the militants diving for cover, and several men spilled over the side. Suddenly, small arms fire from the smaller building to the right caused Jackson to slide the Little Bird left.

As he straightened out to fire, several bullets tagged the side of the cockpit. The thumps startled the pilots, but Jackson responded by dipping the nose and firing two of its 70mm rockets into the rooftop. He accelerated forward, directly in the wake of the ensuing explosions, and raked the militants with more mini gunfire. By wisely changing his tactics, Jackson had avoided becoming a sitting duck.

Through the noise and confusion, Whitely continued to frantically explain the situation to Morgan. "Commander, send air support. I repeat, send air support. We are taking ground fire from approximately thirty gunmen."

"I read you. Get the hell out of there. Stand off, and we'll hit the buildings in about three minutes."

"Yes, sir. Pulling out."

Jackson had just lined up for another run at the two bigger buildings when the command came through. He complied with orders and the helicopter began to rise just as an RPG was fired from somewhere below. The grenade, with its spiraling smoke trail, whizzed by several feet below the cockpit. Jackson and Whitely gave each other a long, wide-eyed look before muttering prayers of thanks for divine intervention.

Chapter Twenty-Five

The air strike had leveled all three buildings in a swift response to the attack on Morgan's men. In the aftermath, Jackson had swooped in under Morgan's orders and fired three rockets into an escaping truck full of militants. A Marine unit arrived minutes later to mop up. They arrested three severely wounded gunmen and shot one crazed fourteen-year-old boy who rushed the soldiers while holding a grenade in each hand.

Buzz and Naseth arrived from the east with an escort of Army Rangers. The small convoy of Humvees passed the scorched hull of the would-be getaway truck and parked past a Marine checkpoint. The agents stepped onto the blackened soil surrounding the militant hideout and took in the devastation. What used to be multi-story buildings had been reduced to fragments of concrete and wood.

Naseth pointed into the rubble. "Is that a body?"

A Marine stood from a crouched position near the center of the pile. "Affirmative, sir. Nice and crispy. There's about forty of 'em in the rock piles."

"Forty dead?"

"Yes, sir."

Lieutenant Colonel Morgan approached from behind. "They're probably Iraqis. We have reports that foreigners are coming in, but I would never expect to see such a large group in one place. They tend not to congregate. This is a good example why they don't."

Buzz shook his head, a little overwhelmed by all the carnage. "We caught an Iraqi lieutenant who told me their soldiers were given orders to break up into smaller squads if their positions were overrun."

Morgan squatted and picked up a small charred bone fragment to analyze. "I know that's how the Fedayeen operate. But I haven't heard any reports about regular army units following the same tactics."

"That's because we're still feeding our intelligence through the usual channels. It has to filter down."

"Huh, figures. Block's right there in the other room, but you guys won't tell him anything that might save soldiers' lives. I nearly had two pilots shot out of the sky trying to catch your suspects. Seems like the CIA could skip the middle men and keep us in the loop."

Buzz could only look around and nod in agreement. "I did tell you our suspects were headed to Mosul, though. Should get a little credit for that."

"True. Well, even if your prisoner is telling the truth, the order to break up and start a guerrilla war may not have reached every Iraqi soldier. Or they may have decided to ignore orders by now—too much chaos at this point. I just don't believe these were foreigners."

"We informed agent Reid of this incident," Naseth interjected. "She's checking her field reports to see if we stirred any activity inside Mosul. Should help us determine who they were."

"The CIA already has assets in Mosul?"

"Yes, sir. Hey, I spent weeks on surveillance inside Basrah myself. I learned a lot about what was going on in the buildup before the war just by watching and listening. We'll have new information soon enough."

Something distracted Buzz as his partner extolled the virtues of the CIA. Naseth, noticing him panning the surroundings, tried to figure out what was bothering him, but came up empty. "What's wrong?"

Instead of answering, Buzz wandered off in the direction of a young Marine who stood alone in the middle of the road, examining its surface. Naseth shrugged his shoulders and Morgan offered no explanation. "Agent Naseth, I'm going to get my boys out of here. Looks like the Marines can wrap this up."

"Thanks, Commander. Good luck with your mission."

They shook hands and parted ways. On Morgan's signal, the Rangers loaded up and moved out. Naseth caught up to the tall Texan, closely examining the road's surface as they approached the curious Marine.

Buzz nodded to the baby-faced soldier. "Private, I'm Special Agent Foster with the CIA. Call me Buzz."

"Hello, sir. Private Jeff Rodriguez."

"I noticed you looking at something here."

"Oh, just curious, sir. I'm supposed to be patrolling for survivors."

"That's fine. I'm not here to get you in trouble. Just tell me what you see."

"It's nothing, sir. Not part of my assignment."

"Tell me anyway. I'd like any information that might help. Nothing is too small to overlook."

Rodriguez glanced repeatedly at his commander who, for the moment, was too busy to notice. "Well, I saw these black trails coming out of the scorched sand. They look like blackened dirt." Rodriguez kicked the tracks to illustrate his point. "If you follow them back off the road, they look like tire tracks. Go all the way back to that carport behind the bigger building. At least I think it was a carport."

"I see. So you think a car drove through the sand after the bombs scorched it?"

"Looks like it to me, sir. Looks like someone escaped straight towards Mosul."

"Sounds like a good bet. Nice work."

Rodriguez shook his hand proudly, but tensed at the sight of his commanding officer approaching in a typical bad mood.

"Private Rodriguez! What are you doing, son?"

Buzz let go of the soldier's hand. "Sir, I'm with the CIA and this man just pointed out we have at least one vehicle that escaped the air strike."

The commander lightened up immediately. "Is that so? You think he's right?"

"Yes, sir. I know he is."

"Well, son, maybe you should be promoted, not scolded." The commander patted Rodriguez on the back.

"Do you mind if I borrow him?" Buzz asked.

"Sure, as long as you don't take off with him."

"We'll keep him close, sir," Buzz promised.

The commander patted his Marine again, then returned to his men, who were still sifting through the rubble.

When the commander was out of earshot, Naseth finally broke his silence. "Buzz, what do you have in mind?"

"Get in touch with Reid. Tell her we had a vehicle escape the air strike heading west toward Mosul. We need an update on any strange movements in town. Rodriguez here is going to search for license plates."

"License plates, sir?"

"Yep. Bring me every plate you can find on all the charred trucks and cars."

"So you have a license plate number already?"

"That's right. If it's not here, then our suspects' car got out. Now get going." As Rodriguez walked off to search for plates, Buzz added, "Afterwards, we're gonna talk about your plans after the Marine Corps."

When Buzz turned back to Naseth, he was arguing with Reid over the phone. The pressure was building as they sensed their suspects had slipped through once again. It seemed as if the painted man, the ultimate target of the Army and CIA investigation, had become a ghost, constantly fading from their grasp.

Chapter Twenty-Six

Two nearly identical middle-aged men wearing identical suits waited at a red light in their government issued car. The driver, Special Agent Rick Tiller, tapped the steering wheel impatiently. His partner, Don Veron, laughed and shook his head. "How'd you ever get into the FBI? You have the worst case of road rage I've ever seen."

"Hey, I never asked to transfer to Houston, Texas. My God, the drivers here are idiots!"

"What do you want from her? It's a red light. Besides, drivers everywhere are idiots."

"Look at her yackin' away on that phone. She has no clue what's going on around her. And what's with this light? Turn green, damn it!"

"Five bucks says she goes within three seconds of the light turning green."

"You're on."

They waited and the light turned green. She did not budge until the signal changed to yellow. The car lurched forward slightly and the woman kept talking on her phone as if nothing had happened. Tiller unbuckled his seatbelt and shifted into park.

"Rick? Where're you going? Don't do this again, Rick!"

Veron watched helplessly from the passenger seat as his partner, red-faced and itching to vent, walked to the driver side window of the lady's car and flashed his credentials. She immediately pulled the phone away from her ear and rolled down the window. Tiller reached in and, astonishingly, grabbed her cell phone. She sat passively as he tossed the phone over her car into a field.

As he walked back, the lady, stunned by Veron's gall, took a right turn and parked against the curb. Moments later, the signal changed to green again and Tiller happily accelerated into the intersection.

"Feel better?"

"Much."

Tiller spent the rest of the trip into the Houston suburbs whistling. The traffic no longer bothered him, but now his partner had to patiently endure Tiller's merrier side. Finally, they found the apartment complex they were searching for and both agents quickly focused on the task at hand.

Some of the buildings in the complex had numbers, and others did not. Agents Tiller and Veron, both seasoned professionals, methodically worked through the complex until they found apartment number 232 on the second floor. Veron tapped on the rusty metal door. "Hasan, open up. FBI."

Inside, Hasan jumped to his feet and nervously fixed on the front door. He had been immersed in a CNN marathon of Iraq war coverage for most of the day. Now, suddenly, the U.S. government was standing at his doorstep. Considering his family tree, Hasan suspected that this might happen. All the government needed to kick him out of the country was to find any potential immigration issues. And Hasan had a mound of troubles stemming from the typical red tape he constantly fought.

As the pounding and yelling escalated, Hasan grew more certain they intended to arrest him. He frantically grabbed pants and shoes, hastily dressing himself.

Outside, Tiller grabbed Veron's wrist, preventing him from knocking again. On cue, each man pressed an ear against the door.

"I hear something," Tiller said, almost as a question.

"Yeah, I hear it. You hear that?"

"Sounded like a sliding door! He's going off the balcony!"

Veron pounded violently this time. "Hasan! We're not here to arrest you! We just need your help!"

Tiller took off for the stairs. "I'm going to cut him off! Go on in!"

Veron backed away from the door, then leveled a solid kick just above the knob. After a second attempt, the panel busted and the door flung wide open, slamming hard against the wall. He drew his 9mm, but quickly realized Hasan was no threat. The tiny Iraqi had stepped over the balcony railing and was scanning the ground for a soft spot to land.

Veron sprinted to the glass sliding door and tried to open it. He made several attempts before noticing a wooden pole wedged against the door on the outside. Hasan had slithered down the railing by the time Veron returned from the kitchen with a chair, which he used to smash through the door. As the glass fell, Hasan hung precariously from the balcony by his fingertips. Veron rushed outside, quickly bent over the railing, and grabbed Hasan's hands.

"Hasan, we just need your help. It's about your brother."

"I knew it would come! You want me out of America because of my brother!"

"No, no! Please, just let us talk to you!"

Hasan struggled to hold on, but his face reddened, and his knuckles turned white. Veron reached lower, but Hasan's fingers slipped, and he lost his grip completely.

Tiller rounded the corner of the building as Hasan crashed to the soft grass below. The two-story drop did not seem like much, but he landed awkwardly. Still, his desperation overcame the limitations of his injury.

Hasan ran with a pronounced limp toward a small fenced-in swimming pool. He opened the waist-high gate and staggered inside. But Tiller closed in too fast. He leaped over the fence and crashed into the smaller, slower Hasan. Both men stumbled precariously forward to the edge of the pool.

Hasan's sore leg folded under the pressure, sending him head over heals into a sludge of algae covering the water. Amazingly, Tiller caught his balance just before following Hasan into the water. Unfortunately, Hasan appeared to be unconscious. He would have to get wet after all. Tiller threw off his jacket and gun while screaming at his partner. "Veron! Get down here, fast!"

Veron laughed as Veron dove in after Hasan. He just hoped he could save him and avoid an investigation. Both agents hated desk duty.

Chapter Twenty-Seven

Several industrial buildings stood at the south end of the Mosul airfield. Obviously, they had seen their fair share of combat. The largest, a three-story structure with outside covered walkways encircling each level, was pockmarked with holes. The damage seemed likely the result of tank rounds, but the surrounding warehouses had clearly been bombed from the sky.

The railroad tracks to the west provided the perfect observation point for Buzz and Naseth. From a parked railcar, Naseth watched the large, mostly intact building. He paid particular attention to the third-floor balcony where two men had been seen periodically stepping out for smoke breaks. Both carried AK-47's strapped to their backs. Neither gunman looked familiar, but Reid had assured Naseth the suspects were here. The car had been identified on its way into town by Reid's informant. After ditching the vehicle, the suspects from Agrah met five Sunni militants who brought them here.

Buzz grabbed the binoculars as the two smokers stepped out again. "Same two. Guess they're the only ones in there who smoke."

Naseth scanned the area behind their position. The locals milled around sporadically, but nothing seemed out of the ordinary. "I've watched these Iraqis for awhile now. Most of them don't go outside unless they have a reason. Those two are lookouts. Most likely they're watching from inside, but come out when something looks a little suspicious. The smoking is just a cover."

"Well, Reid said there were at least five gunmen besides our two suspects. Probably got a few watching the other side," Buzz suggested.

"Safe to say," Naseth said. "Why don't we call in the Army? We're pretty sure these are some bad guys, and our suspects are probably in there."

The smokers headed back inside. Buzz surveyed the rest of the building. "Well, we don't know for sure they're in there. If soldiers come lobbing tank rounds, it might just scare 'em off before we catch 'em. Gotta identify them personally first."

"But you do agree that you and I aren't going in alone. There's too many of them."

Buzz flashed a mischievous grin while fitting his pistol with a silencer.

"Come on Buzz. You've got to be kidding."

"Why do you think I borrowed this thing?"

Naseth followed Buzz's finger to the sniper rifle leaning against the crates. "You don't expect me to use that?" Naseth asked.

"Why not? It's only in case I need cover fire."

"Buzz, I'm not ready for this. You saw me freeze up. If I had pulled the trigger in Agrah, we wouldn't be here."

"Look, get the transmitter out of the bag and set it up. You'll be able to monitor everything. I'm just gonna try and get in there to confirm it's them. I'll get out when I've seen 'em, and then we'll call in the cavalry. Your job will be to watch for any strange movements and just shoot anybody who might be trying to shoot me."

Naseth hesitantly prepared his equipment and handed Buzz an earpiece. "What if the place is full of gunmen?"

"Then I'll find out soon enough." Buzz scooted across to the backside of the railcar and transformed himself into a local. "Look buddy, I'm not worried about what happened in Agrah. You're a professional. You won't let me down."

Naseth nodded slowly, then grabbed the sniper rifle. Buzz patted him on the shoulder and jumped to the ground. The building had no guards outside for the moment, but Naseth knew they were watching. "Buzz, you read me?"

"Uh huh. Going in on the right side entrance. You'll see me in a few minutes."

"Good, I'm calling Reid. Making the Army aware of our position. I'll have them stand off until we're ready for them."

"Uh huh."

"I'll take that as approval."

"Uh huh."

Naseth dialed while positioning the rifle. "Reid, it's Naseth. Get us a unit in place to take down the building we talked about. Buzz is entering to identify our suspects. I'll call to confirm he's out of the building." He paused, then added, "I know he's crazy. If you wanted a sane boyfriend, you should have picked a nice accountant." He paused again. "Hey now, that was uncalled for. Wait, there he is. I'll call back. Over and out."

Buzz approached the building from the right, blending in with the locals, though abnormally tall. From his vantage point, Buzz knew Naseth could not see the entrance on that side of the building. But something there caught Buzz's eye. He stopped and stared in that direction, knowing his transmitter was picking up voices in the

143

background for Naseth's benefit. Unfortunately, Buzz's Arabic sounded too American, so he merely held his arms up and shrugged.

"Buzz, are you OK?" Naseth asked.

"Uh uh." The response was barely audible.

Naseth watched as Buzz stepped forward, then disappeared behind the corner of the building. Naseth could hear the voices growing louder, ordering Buzz to drop to his knees. A pause followed. Then Naseth heard three abbreviated sounds, unmistakably that of silenced pistol shots. Naseth grabbed the rifle and watched the corner of the building through the scope. An unidentified man staggered away from the building, dropped his AK-47, and fell to the ground.

Buzz stepped from obscurity and grabbed the dead man's legs. As he dragged the body out of sight, Naseth made sure the shooting had not aroused interest. "Buzz, I don't see any other movement. You OK?"

"I'm good. Going inside."

Naseth lowered the rifle and tried to relax. After a few moments of relative silence, he spoke into his transmitter. "Buzz, if you can hear me, the smokers are outside again. They're looking a little more concerned than usual. One of them is talking on a radio, and they're scanning the grounds pretty thoroughly."

A response never came, only the muffled sounds of Buzz's movements. Naseth tightened his grip on the rifle and waited for the gunmen on the balcony to make a move. From such a distance, he could not hear them screaming at each other, but he surmised they had lost contact with the guard Buzz had just eliminated. After a

heated exchange, one of the gunmen ran inside the
building, leaving only the one man for Naseth to handle.

"Buzz, I know you can hear me. Get out of there now!
They know something's wrong!"

Naseth put the lone militant directly in the crosshairs
of the rifle's scope while waiting to hear from Buzz. It
didn't take long for voices to start filtering through the
transmitter as Buzz seemed to stop moving. The voices
grew louder, and Naseth could clearly understand the
Arabic now. They were looking for an intruder.

"Buzz, you heard that. Get out."

The screaming militants inside grew in number and
sounded like they were mere feet away. At least four
distinct voices could be heard, not including the warbled
voices coming from the radios. Then, all of a sudden, the
yelling stopped completely, followed by the punctuated
sounds of a silenced pistol. After the third shot, the
shouting resumed at a frantic pace. From the transmitter,
and simultaneously from a distance, bursts of gunfire
signaled that Buzz had been discovered.

The man on the balcony was not alone for long. Six
other gunmen streamed out to investigate. Naseth
remained well concealed, but not very helpful. With the
safety engaged, he went through the motions of
eliminating the men on the balcony. Several scenarios
played out in his mind, but he weighed the
unpredictability of a gun battle. Once the first man fell, the
other five could react in any number of ways. And he was
far from a crack shot at any distance.

"Buzz, six armed men on the front balcony! Not a
good exit point!"

The gunfire continued, but Buzz decided to answer this time. "That's the only way I'm getting out. I'm gonna blow the front door with a grenade I borrowed from one of our former friends. Another explosion will follow. On that second explosion, start taking out those guards. Keep 'em busy."

"Affirmative!" Naseth barked into his radio.

Naseth nervously readied his weapon while the gunmen spread out across the third-floor balcony. His task had just increased in difficulty. As promised, the front door splintered outward into a mangled mess, accompanied, a moment later, by a loud blast. A second grenade exploded inside and, on cue, Naseth sprung into action. This time he did not hesitate. Starting with the gunmen farthest to his left, he fired rounds moving methodically to his right.

The first shot missed its mark, but due to the commotion below, and the silencer attached to the rifle's barrel, no one noticed. The gunman fell with the second bullet. Naseth hit the next militant with one shot and quickly moved to the third. Unfortunately, this one had seen the fate of his two partners, even through the confusion. Naseth fired, but sent the bullet over the man's head as he ducked at just the right moment.

The gunman jerked around when the wall behind him splintered from the bullet's impact. Then the son-of-a-bitch screamed a warning to the others. Buzz made his way through the opening in the front doors, tossing his last grenade inside. Naseth saw him start running just as the railcar began taking automatic weapons fire.

Buzz never slowed down and the men on the balcony quickly spotted him. A barrage of bullets rained down on him, but Naseth kept firing just enough to buy Buzz the time he needed to reach the railcar. As Naseth watched, Buzz rounded the corner and dove, head first, behind the antiquated boxcar.

The gun battle grew louder, causing the people in the streets behind the tracks to run for cover. When he was settled, Buzz reached around and felt a bullet wound in the back of his left shoulder, deciding to ignore it for now. He poked his head under the boxcar, taking in the melee' on the other side. Four men lay dead on the balcony, but reinforcements had replaced them and then some. There appeared to be at least seven men, with more joining them from inside the building.

The most recent addition to the balcony held an RPG launcher. Buzz thought that this might be a good time to make his exit. He stood and slid the side door open, then glanced back, signaling for Naseth to follow. Out of the corner of his eye, Buzz saw his partner's motionless body lying slumped over the rifle. Cold sweat started to bead his brow as he slowly realized he would have to go alone. Though the bullets kept coming, Buzz jumped back into the railcar and checked his friend's pulse. As he held Naseth's wrist, his worst fears were confirmed. But he had no time to mourn, only the will to survive.

Buzz grabbed the rifle and satellite phone before making a hasty departure. Once on the ground, he found the closest building and started running. His instincts and timing could not have been better. Moments into his escape, the railcar exploded. Unfortunately, Naseth's body would never be recovered.

Buzz mentally played back his decision to enter the building in a guilt ridden tug-of-war with himself as he dialed for Army support. "Reid, our suspects are inside, but you better take down the building—quick."

"They know you're there?"

"I'd say so, and there's a lot more than five guys in there! More like dozens!"

"Hold on!"

Buzz watched from a safe distance as the railcar burned and bad guys with guns swarmed the grounds. Then the helicopters came and drilled more holes into the side of the tattered building in a lethal rain of fifty caliber rounds. The men on the balcony danced like puppets as bullets riddled their bodies.

"Buzz? You there?"

"I'm here. Watching the show."

"What's wrong? Are you hurt?"

Buzz patted his bloody shoulder. "No, I'm fine."

"It's Naseth, isn't it? What happened?" Reid asked.

"I'm sorry, I couldn't even get his body out of there." A pause followed as tanks and Bradley fighting vehicles encircled the compound.

"Buzz, I'm sorry."

"Not nearly as sorry as I am."

"You should come to the camp. I'll talk to Holt about getting you a ride."

"I'll call you once I follow up here. Got a score to settle."

"Buzz, I'm ordering you to let the Army take care of the details. You get back here as soon as possible—you understand?"

"Like I said, I'll call you." He disconnected before she could argue. The Army continued pounding the building, turning it into so much smoldering rubble, and along with it any trace of his fallen partner. Buzz forced the regrets out of his head. He could only focus on catching his suspects, for his friend's sake.

Chapter Twenty-Eight

Hashimi kept busy in a number of ways, passing time better than the other prisoners held at Camp Slayer. He had found the entertainment building where soldiers played pool and listened to music between patrols. His escort, a square-jawed MP, always followed at a fair distance, allowing him some measure of privacy. Though Hashimi had trouble getting a game at first, his propensity for revealing potential Iraqi hideouts quickly made him friends.

The patrols would come in after following up on one of his tips and tell him all about the weapons caches or rebel fighters they had found. At least one unit commander lobbied Block to have the ankle bracelet removed, and his escort assigned to other duties. Of course, Block knew that by playing nice, Hashimi might land a full pardon and a release back into the population of his own country. Block did not fully trust Hashimi and kept him under guard.

As the daylight faded, Hashimi ventured outdoors to pursue one of his favorite pastimes. With a little ingenuity, and supplies that he'd gathered from various soldiers, he had fashioned a suitable fishing pole. Now he stood at the water's edge, baiting his hook with pieces of hot dog, and casting into a calm, shallow area of the river. The MP nervously checked his watch, but had grown a little to lax with his charge. He allowed Hashimi extra time against his better judgment.

The peaceful sounds of birds and rustling leaves were occasionally interrupted by the muffled sounds of battles raging in the distance. Hashimi pondered the fate of his country and lost track of time. The darkness of night slowly enveloped him, but he remained oblivious until the nearby shuffling of feet snapped him out of his daydream.

The silhouette of a limping woman approached the riverbank and Hashimi immediately recognized agent Reid. He pulled in his line, then turned to meet her, but stopped short when he heard faint sobs. "Hashimi? Is that you?"

"Yes, Reid. I am sorry. I will leave you."

"No, no. Come on over."

As she came into view, Hashimi could see wetness on her cheeks glimmer in the dim lights of the opposite shore. He reluctantly joined her as she wiped away tears. "Did something happen to Buzz?"

Reid leaned against the railing overlooking the water. "No, Buzz is fine, but another agent was killed."

"I am sorry to hear this."

"His name is Mark Naseth."

"I see him. He looks like an Arab. He reads the skin writings."

Reid took a breath. "That's right, you met him."

"It is a shame to see people die. I pray for him tonight."

Reid appreciated the sentiment, but noticed something strange in his demeanor, as if he were merely humoring her.

Suddenly, Reid straightened. In her grief, she had forgotten who and where she was. "Why are you helping us so much?" she asked tentatively.

"What do you mean by this?"

"I mean, you've been very helpful." She stared at him for a long moment, then asked, "What motive could you possibly have other than to help yourself out of trouble?"

"It is true, I do not like jail. It is important to me to help my country. It does not help Iraq to keep fighting."

"You don't really care about Americans though—whether we live or die."

"We all die. It is important to die with honor. This agent Naseth dies with honor, so I pray for him. It does not matter if he is American."

Reid watched him.

Hashimi scratched at the skin under his electronic ankle bracelet. "The man that looks like Duri. Who is this man?" Hashimi asked, changing the subject.

"General Duri, as far as we know," Reid said. She regarded the Iraqi with nagging doubts, but decided to play along. "They found his brother back in the States and we're running DNA tests on both of them."

"Ah, just like your cop shows. This is a good thing to do, I think. But I tell you, it is not Duri."

"You have a lot of hatred for him, don't you?"

"Yes, much hate."

"Then you would help us find the General if he's still out there, right?"

Hashimi turned and looked her squarely in the eyes. "Yes, I help."

Reid's satellite phone cut the conversation short. "Excuse me, that's Buzz." She turned and walked back into the darkness.

Hashimi excused himself to no one in particular. He collected his pole and vowed to try fishing again in the morning.

* * *

Buzz stood a safe distance behind a squad of soldiers screaming into an open door leading to the building's basement. The soldiers shouted orders in English and Arabic, but the militants at the bottom of the staircase refused to give up. Occasionally, a burst of gunfire from below temporarily halted the yelling.

He finished briefing Reid and disconnected the phone. The soldiers started shouting again, but Buzz had heard enough. He tapped the squad leader on the shoulder. "Corporal, I don't care anymore if they live or die! This is too dangerous!"

"OK, agent Foster. We'll try to maintain good trigger control so we don't make too much of a mess. We might even be able to keep from killing whoever it is you're looking for."

"I'd appreciate that!"

The corporal gave his orders and his men tossed three flash bang grenades through the doorway. Following the triple concussion, the men filed down the stairs two-by-two, through the smoke into the darkness. Two shots followed and then, nothing.

Buzz crept up to the doorway, but could see nothing without the night vision goggles the soldiers sported. Once the ringing in his ears stopped, all he could hear was mumbling and the moans of an injured man. Then the corporal invited him down. "Agent Foster, you better get in here!"

"How 'bout some light?"

"You got it!"

Buzz descended the stairs slowly as a pair of medics nearly ran him down from behind. When he reached the bottom, they were frantically administering CPR to one of the suspects. The man's shirt was drenched in blood. The heavy copper smell made Buzz nauseous. With the aid of a multitude of green glow sticks, Buzz recognized him as Ayad, the older man from Agrah, Darin Helton's murderer.

"Don't let him die! I haven't had a shot at the bastard yet!"

The medics ignored the comment and continued working. Buzz looked around and found a hole in the wall just beyond a dead militant. The corporal was standing there, examining the tunnel entrance and shining a flashlight at the ground for Buzz to see. "Looks like a blood trail. Leads from upstairs down to here."

"And it goes all the way into the tunnel?"

"Yep. We confirmed that three men came down, and, as you can see, one's dead and one's dying."

"And the third is injured. Let's hope it's his leg."

"I've already called in the dogs," the corporal said. "We'll go in as soon as they get here."

"Good job, Corporal. I'll stay with this guy. Gotta get him back to the camp whether he lives or dies."

The medics stopped CPR, then injected antibiotics into Ayad. He was still breathing, but just barely. Soon, they were able to pick him up and carry him hastily up the stairs with Buzz close behind. On their way to an awaiting helicopter, a squad of soldiers entered through the hole in the front doors behind three anxious German shepherds. They strained and pulled on their leashes, up on their haunches, teeth bared. Buzz hoped they were hungry.

Chapter Twenty-Nine

The helicopter landed at Camp Slayer in the courtyard near the infirmary. Unfortunately for Buzz, a welcoming party waited. He wanted no part of a conversation with Block, or an emotional reunion with Reid. He should have known how complex a relationship with her could become, especially in a situation like this—a war zone. In his line of work, emotional attachments had always been complicated, that's why he had so few.

The medics filed out first, then handed off their patient to the Army doctors. Buzz thought he could give Reid the slip, but he never stood a chance. She nearly tackled him before both feet hit the ground. They embraced for a long while before she finally loosened her grip. When their eyes met, Reid's were filled with tears. His seemed empty.

"Listen, Reid. I can't do this right now."

She backed off, clearly upset, but understanding. "You said you weren't hurt." She glanced at his shoulder. "What's with the blood and the hole in your shirt?"

"It's nothing. Bullet went right through." He kissed her on the forehead, then slipped past her and jogged toward the infirmary with Block following eagerly. He had to force himself not to look back.

At that moment, as he walked past her with barely another look, Reid knew they shouldn't work together much longer. They had grown close in such a short time that she didn't really know him. Maybe it had been no more than someone to hold onto while pretending to be oblivious to the nightmare all around them. Or maybe he felt differently about her. Either way, her career had brought her here, and right now, the mission had to supersede any of her personal feelings.

Inside, the doctors prepped for surgery while Buzz watched the suspect's labored breathing. He looked unnaturally blanch, a little waxy, had the look of death. Block walked past the rows of wounded soldiers and leaned over Ayad's gurney.

"Do you recognize him, Colonel?" Buzz asked hopefully.

Block backed away from the suspect and came up alongside Buzz. He smelled like a shower and a fresh shave. "I believe so. I'll have to check our files, but I think he's an officer under Duri's command. Name's Ayad or something like that. Sedal's got a photographic memory. I'll send him in to get a look."

"We have him identified as Ayad Ammash Hasan, so your recollection is pretty good."

Block could see this was not the same man who'd left camp a day before. His clothes were in tatters, his shirt bloodstained, and his hands shook almost imperceptively. "You OK?"

"Why?"

"Hey, war is hell. I know that."

"Yeah, you're right." Buzz glanced down at his feet. When he looked up again, his eyes were red. "He was a good friend. It hurts."

"And he died serving his country," Block said, uncharacteristically without bravado.

"He was doing what I asked him to do, protect me if I got in trouble," Buzz continued.

"And you think you shouldn't have put him in that position."

"That's right."

"Let me tell you something. Somebody had to go in that building. And I don't know too many men with balls enough to do it. He was supporting you, protecting you. And he was proud to do it. I can guarantee you that."

Buzz cracked an uneven smile, then exhaled. They remained silent over the next forty-five minutes while watching the doctors expertly remove the bullet from Ayad's chest. To their surprise, after the surgery, the prognosis looked good. The doctors assured Block that Ayad would be able to talk after a good long rest.

Buzz rubbed his eyes and stretched his aching shoulder. "The bastard's a survivor, I'll give 'em that."

"What about you? You have to get that looked at." Block said.

"Yeah, why not? I'm already here."

"You and Reid are doing a good job of keeping these doctors in business."

"Listen, I think I'd get the General in here as soon as Ayad is able to talk," Buzz said.

"Good idea. Might tell us a few things. We'll bug the room, put up a camera. Let them hang out a little bit."

Block started to walk away, but Buzz caught him by the arm before he took no more than a few steps. "Block," he said in a low voice. "I know about the robot spying on us. Tell Sedal."

The colonel paused momentarily, flashed a nervous grin, then left without saying another word.

Buzz sat on an empty bed and removed his bloody shirt. He felt light headed. His bandages had soaked completely through. He would get medical attention, but more importantly, some much needed rest.

* * *

The morning sun streamed through small mud-caked windows near the ceiling of a dank basement under an abandoned government building. Suddenly, a towering stack of wooden crates and pallets tumbled away from the concrete wall, crashing to the ground, leaving clouds of dust dancing in the shafts of light shining in from outside. As the wood fell, a man emerged from a gap, kicking and shoving his way through the clutter. Rashid, the man who had evaded both Special Forces and special agents, crawled desperately across the pile using only his good arm.

Behind him, he could hear barking dogs echoing in the chambers of the intricate tunnel network beneath the town of Mosul. Rashid stumbled onto the floor and tossed as many pieces of lumber across the opening as possible. Then he fumbled around in the dim light, looking for the stairs. Unfortunately for him, the echo effects of the tunnel caused him to misjudge the distance of his pursuers.

Three angry German shepherds exploded through the poorly blocked opening, heading straight for Rashid, who had just bumped into the staircase railing. He spun around and gaped panic-stricken at the dogs, which seemed to glow from the beams of faded light at their backs. With his good arm, Rashid managed to draw his pistol and fire a shot into the onslaught. He missed the dogs, but the blast scattered the pack, disrupting their charge.

Now his pursuers were obscured by darkness. Rashid fired another random shot, then bounded up the stairs. He nearly made it to the top before the ground-level door swung open. Stunned, Rashid froze temporarily, but after a few seconds, gathered his composure. He raised his pistol toward the silhouette standing at the door, but before he could squeeze the trigger, a gunshot sent a bullet ripping into his right thigh.

Rashid tumbled down the stairs, dropping his gun along the way. The dogs found him one by one, sinking their teeth into various appendages, until they were yanking him in three different directions. His screams rose above the growling and snarling. The dogs would have torn him to shreds if not for the arrival of their handlers, a mass of soldiers, streaming through the tunnel entrance and calling out commands.

As soon as they pulled the dogs off Rashid, the soldiers lit up the area with flashlights and glow sticks, illuminating his bloody body. Before the soldiers had a chance to assess the tattered Iraqi at their feet, sounds from the top of the stairs caused several of them to draw their weapons in that direction. A man slowly stepped down out of the gloom above, hands raised.

"It's OK, CIA," Buzz shouted.

The young corporal, whom he had met at the militant hideout hours before, recognized him. "Weapons down! It's agent Foster!"

Buzz calmly holstered his sidearm and rolled a toothpick between his lips. "Tell the medics to back off."

The corporal looked back over his shoulder at a soldier climbing across the wood pile. "Buzz, this man has to get medical attention. He's bleeding pretty badly."

"Just give me a minute," Buzz flatly demanded as he knelt beside the writhing suspect. He studied the numerous injuries and guessed the fresh bullet wound in his leg would be the most painful. Instead of helping, Buzz added to his misery by clamping down directly on the hole in the flesh.

Rashid's torso sprung forward and he screamed bloody murder. Buzz let up. "Tell me about your tattoos." At first, Rashid started speaking in Arabic, but Buzz had a different idea. "English."

"Yes. Don't hurt me."

"See, I knew you could speak English. The tattoos."

"I truly do not know this word."

"The writings on your skin. Tell me, and we'll give you medicine for your pain."

Rashid closed his eyes and began to speak. "OK, I tell you. They cannot be looked at."

"I know about the light used to read the writings. We found another man. This man had the writings on his skin."

"Yes. Mahmud Jafari. He is not real."

Buzz felt a tinge of excitement. "And what about you?"

"The writings on my skin are real."

"And the General? What do you know about him?"

"He is a bastard. And he has a man who look like him."

"He has a double? Why? Where is this look-alike?"

"Protecting Mahmud. The General gets away for some reason I do not know."

Buzz nodded to the medic, who dropped to one knee and immediately tried to stop the bleeding. The corporal followed Buzz to the other side of the room, away from the suspect. "You didn't happen to bring one of those lights with you, did you?"

"No. We need to get him back to camp as soon as we can. Contact your unit and get a transport."

"How in the hell did you find this place, anyway?"

"A new friend of mine. He knows all about the tunnels. This is the only other entrance to this one."

"You mean all the others just lead to nowhere?"

"Apparently."

"Huh, well, I'll contact my commander and get us out of here."

The corporal checked with the medic, then ordered his men to carry the suspect up the stairs. Rashid groaned as they lifted his tattered body. "Where is medicine for my pain?"

Buzz chuckled. "You know, funny thing. Turns out they don't have any pain meds. My mistake. Maybe the doctors'll have some."

The soldiers stifled laughs as they headed above ground. Despite the jokes at Rashid's expense, he was either the most important man in all of Iraq, or the Army and CIA were about to be embarrassed again, Buzz thought.

Chapter Thirty

A pair of Arabic translators hovered over Rashid's nearly nude body in the glow of the strange light. They had moved him to a private room at the back of the infirmary building and covered the window with layers of black plastic garbage bags. Lieutenant Sedal monitored the men with his laptop set up to transfer preliminary transcripts to Block. The colonel waited patiently in the large command center the Army had set up in the gym.

This time, the information would be independently verified by the CIA, DOD, and Army Intelligence before putting a unit together to investigate. Any potential locations gleaned from an interpretation of Rashid's tattoos would be researched for recent and historical uses, analyzed using available satellite photos, and examined using state-of-the-art technology such as thermal imaging cameras. Colonel Holt had vowed to go into any suspect buildings through a hole in the roof if that would avoid casualties to his men.

In the meantime, Holt had ordered two to four man Special Forces teams to watch any potential WMD sites from a safe distance. He had learned some painful lessons the hard way, and would now take all possible precautions before taking action.

The translators compared their first section of notes, then handed Sedal the notebooks. He immediately started typing. From the door, a menacing old nurse glared at the men. Her job was to keep the patient safe, but truth be told, Sedal could care less whether he lived or died. His task did not depend on Rashid's survival, and he knew the Iraqi had been responsible for the death of a fellow soldier and a CIA agent. On Sedal's orders, several soldiers grabbed Rashid roughly, flipping him over, and tangling wires and IV lines.

The nurse furiously switched on the overhead light. "What the hell are you doing? Get your cotton-picking hands off my patient!"

Sedal continued typing and tried to ignore the scuffle breaking out before him. Despite the confusion, he managed to finish his transcript.

While the soldiers were bouncing him around, Rashid had opened his eyes in bewilderment. His heart monitor sped up and the nurse grew more agitated.

"Leave him for now," Sedal ordered. "Take the notebooks and double-check everything you have so far. Make sure there are no inconsistencies. Nurse, go ahead and give him a sedative. I'll send in the guard."

"Do I look like a damn doctor?" the nurse said indignantly. "I can't give him any drugs!"

"Fine, do whatever you need to do," replied Sedal. "If it were up to me, he'd die slowly and painfully for what he's done."

Sedal closed up shop, then headed for the main room. Ayad had come out of his coma in an adjacent room, and General Duri would be on his way in soon. Sedal would need to assure that the meeting was recorded for later analysis. At the moment, he was wishing he could clone himself.

A pair of Arabic translators hovered over Rashid's nearly nude body in the glow of the strange light. They had moved him to a private room at the back of the infirmary building and covered the window with layers of black plastic garbage bags. Lieutenant Sedal monitored the men with his laptop set up to transfer preliminary transcripts to Block. The colonel waited patiently in the large command center the Army had set up in the gym.

This time, the information would be independently verified by the CIA, DOD, and Army Intelligence before putting a unit together to investigate. Any potential locations gleaned from an interpretation of Rashid's tattoos would be researched for recent and historical uses, analyzed using available satellite photos, and examined using state-of-the-art technology such as thermal imaging cameras. Colonel Holt had vowed to go into any suspect buildings through a hole in the roof if that would avoid casualties to his men.

In the meantime, Holt had ordered two to four-man Special Forces teams to watch any potential WMD sites from a safe distance. He had learned some painful lessons the hard way, and would now take all possible precautions before taking action.

The translators compared their first section of notes, then handed Sedal the notebooks. He immediately started typing. From the door, a menacing old nurse glared at the men. Her job was to keep the patient safe, but truth be told, Sedal could care less whether he lived or died. His task did not depend on Rashid's survival, and he knew the Iraqi had been responsible for the death of a fellow soldier and a CIA agent. On Sedal's orders, several soldiers grabbed Rashid roughly, flipping him over, and tangling wires and IV lines.

The nurse furiously switched on the overhead light. "What the hell are you doing? Get your cotton-picking hands off my patient!"

Sedal continued typing and tried to ignore the scuffle breaking out before him. Despite the confusion, he managed to finish his transcript.

While the soldiers were bouncing him around, Rashid had opened his eyes in bewilderment. His heart monitor sped up and the nurse grew more agitated.

"Leave him for now," Sedal ordered. "Take the notebooks and double-check everything you have so far. Make sure there are no inconsistencies. Nurse, go ahead and give him a sedative. I'll send in the guard."

"Do I look like a damn doctor?" the nurse said indignantly. "I can't give him any drugs!"

"Fine, do whatever you need to do," replied Sedal. "If it were up to me, he'd die slowly and painfully for what he's done."

Sedal closed up shop, then headed for the main room. Ayad had come out of his coma in an adjacent room, and General Duri would be on his way in soon. Sedal would need to assure that the meeting was recorded for later analysis. At the moment, he was wishing he could clone himself.

* * *

The main room of the infirmary had been cleared of all patients except one. Ayad lay quietly in the back corner, suspicious of the recent activity that had left him alone amongst rows of empty hospital cots. It seemed to him that the nurse had been ordered to stay in the back of the building with other patients. Of even greater concern was that the doctors had cut off Ayad's pain medicine hours

165

earlier. Although he felt more lucid, the burning in his chest made the trade-off seem far from fair.

The sounds of his heart monitor and the droning of an outside generator were all that Ayad could hear in the large room. But before the incessant beeping and groaning drove him crazy, a visitor appeared at the front doorway. At that distance in the dimly lit room, Ayad could only guess the man's identity.

The imposing figure shuffled slowly forward, clanking with every step. Behind him, two men in military dress shadowed the heavily shackled prisoner. Ayad sat up in his bed, straining for a better look. As General Duri stepped out of the shadows, Ayad froze. The beeps from his heart monitor sped up as Duri scanned the surroundings. He looked as arrogant as a person could with hands and feet shackled.

The MPs made sure the chains were secure, then walked back to the front door to stand guard. "So, you had some fun with the U.S. military," Duri said, speaking in Arabic. "I also played with them for some time before they captured me. But you do not look so good, my friend."

"You sound bad too," Ayad said mockingly.

"Ah, they have tortured me for the last day. My ribs are broken and my muscles are weak from the electrocution. But I have told them nothing."

Reid listened and watched the video feed on Sedal's computer in the main palace. The lieutenant had left her there to take a break from his heavy workload. She smiled to herself; she had everything she needed. He had shown her the volume control and told her to touch nothing else.

For several minutes, Duri and Ayad talked like they were old friends. Then the mood changed.

The General leaned in and whispered something into Ayad's ear, which was completely inaudible to the microphones. Reid quickly leaned forward and fumbled with the computer mouse, managing to increase the volume to its maximum level. The old man's eyes widened and Duri pulled away, just slightly. Ayad's lips quivered. Reid strained, but could hear nothing more than a low murmur.

Despite the camera's clear zoomed view of both prisoners, Reid could not read lips. She could, however, read body language. Whatever Duri had said scared the hell out of Ayad. And the old man's answer infuriated Duri, that was clear. The assumption that these two old colleagues might just exchange friendly conversation and compare notes turned out to have been optimistic. Reid tried desperately to contact the guards, but she had no idea where Sedal put the radio.

Reid watched helplessly as the situation quickly deteriorated. Duri lunged forward, clamping his shackled hands around Ayad's throat. Ayad's heart monitor accelerated as the frail old man struggled futilely. The MPs, seeing the scuffle, sprinted across the room and pounced hard on Duri, who could not fight back. His sore ribs and weakened muscles failed him. He collapsed to the ground under the soldiers' weight and screamed in agony. For good measure, the larger of the two soldiers put a knee directly into the side of Duri's head, immediately knocking him unconscious.

Unfortunately, by the time the soldiers were able to get Duri off, Ayad, the old man, had flat-lined. Doctors and nurses rushed in and tried desperately to save Ayad's life, but his age and condition worked against him.

Once Reid recovered from the shock of seeing Ayad killed on the laptop right in front of her, she frantically searched the computer room until, finally, she found a radio. "This is agent Reid. Is anyone there?"

Block answered through the static. "Go ahead, agent Reid."

"You better get to the infirmary quick. I think Duri just killed Ayad."

"Damn it! Where's Sedal?"

"He left me to monitor the conversation," she said breathlessly.

"Why the hell would he leave?"

"He's gotta sleep sometime."

"I know—shit! Meet me there."

Reid stared blankly around the room after switching off the radio. She wondered where Buzz had gone after returning from Mosul earlier in the day. She decided not to bother him. He still seemed distant and hurt over the loss of a good friend and did not need any more bad news. She would eventually need to approach him about the incident in Mosul, either as his superior, or as a confidant. There were unresolved issues about his ability to do his job effectively. But for now, she would leave him alone while she cleaned up the latest mess.

Chapter Thirty-One

The entertainment building at Camp Slayer hosted a
steady stream of tired soldiers resting from patrols and
raids. Most played pool or ping-pong on tables collected
from the various palace complex buildings. Others sat
playing checkers or dominoes. Buzz was drinking beer
alone on an uncomfortable stool at a bar usually reserved
for officers.

Sedal watched him from the doorway, debating
whether or not to bother him. Buzz seemed content
drinking alone for the moment, but Sedal knew he would
want the latest information on the case. After all, nobody
was more heavily invested than Buzz in this wild goose
chase.

Through blurred red eyes, Buzz caught a glimpse of
the lieutenant and waved him over with a tired hand.
Surprised, Sedal straightened his glasses, then joined him
at the bar. "Hey Buzz, little early to start drinking."

"Negative, Lieutenant. Never too early. Have a seat.
I'll get you a beer."

"No, that's OK."

"Come on. We're drinkin' to Special Agent Mark
Naseth, who died courageously in the line of duty."

Turning, Buzz picked up a familiar black device on the
bar.

"In that case, I will have a drink," Sedal said.

Sedal glanced at the object Buzz held in his hand.
"That's the remote to the PackBot."

Buzz shot Sedal a quick wink, "Indeed it is. I'm tired,
so PackBot here is going for the beers—just in case they
explode."

169

Sedal heard the robot's tracks suddenly squeal from behind the bar as Buzz directed its movements. He adeptly opened the refrigerator, grabbed two beer bottles, closed the door, and brought them to the bar. The robotic arm extended upward, carefully setting the bottles in front of Sedal.

"Impressive. Now, how about getting it to bring me a bottle opener?"

Buzz smiled like a kid at Christmas. "I was hoping you'd ask. Watch this."

The robotic arm clamped tight on the bottle closest to Sedal. Then another extension rose from the platform below and presented a bottle opener that had been welded to the metal arm. Buzz directed the opener to pop the top, spilling a little beer in the process.

"Oops. Have to work on my technique a little more."

"What did you do to my PackBot?"

"Oh, you mean that USB connection you had on there? Couldn't for the life of me imagine what you'd use that for," Buzz said sarcastically. "Thought I'd modify it a little, make it more useful."

"Well, I can see where your priorities are," Sedal shot back.

Buzz slammed the remote down and swept up his beer in an exaggerated motion. He nearly missed his mouth, but managed to down half the bottle in an angry swig. "You'll have to excuse me, Lieutenant, if I try to relax a spell. I've had a bad couple of days. Productive, but bad. I've killed and captured some bad guys, got shot, and what was that other thing? Oh yeah, I managed to get a very good friend killed. Pardon me for letting off some steam."

Buzz finished his beer and sent the PackBot back to the fridge. Its new mission: keep the beer coming. Sedal ducked his head, then exhaled a long, slow breath. He too was under stress, but his own problems paled next to the misery Buzz was wrestling with. He picked up his beer and drank the entire bottle before stopping for air. Buzz cracked a tired grin and sent the PackBot for two replacements.

"I'm sorry about the comment, Buzz. I've been very busy. It's easy to forget what you've faced."

The robot removed the tops with surprising precision this time. Sedal noticed that the more inebriated Buzz became, the better his motor skills. He grabbed his beer and raised it in a smooth arc toward Buzz. "To agent Naseth."

Buzz clanked his bottle in return. They drank in silence for several minutes, listening to the soldiers laughing and sharing stories. Finally, Sedal asked, "So, how'd you know I was spying on you?"

Buzz laughed, forcing beer out in a spatter. "Oh no, you first. Tell me something I don't know, and I'll tell you a secret."

"Fair enough. We got the results of a DNA test we ran on our General Duri. A couple of Feds ran down a known relative of his back in the States. Poor guy thought it was immigration and nearly got himself killed trying to escape. But they managed to keep him alive, as well as getting a blood sample."

"And?"

"And the tests matched. He's the real deal."

Although he had expected confirmation of Duri's identity, the news confused Buzz. "That's not what I wanted to hear, Lieutenant."

"Why not? At least we know who we got," Sedal said, a little puzzled.

"But what about Hashimi?" Buzz asked.

"I think the General may be playing head games with him." Sedal sensed Buzz's skepticism. "You know, I don't know if I'm supposed to tell you this, but we actually knew about Hashimi before the war even started. Even talked to him by email."

"What the hell?" Buzz blurted.

"No kidding. Before the war started, Army officials made attempts to contact Iraqi officials by email, trying to convince them to surrender. We thought that if we could get even a fraction of the leadership to leave their commands, then chaos would follow in the rank and file."

"That's no secret. Heard that on CNN," Buzz sniped.

"Right. Hashimi was one of the few who responded. That's how we found the bunker where he was hiding."

"How do you explain his story? The fact that he was supposed to escape through the tunnel before the General took his place."

"Easy. That was the original plan—for him not to be there. The whole operation was set up to capture the General. Hashimi wasn't supposed to be there," Sedal repeated. "He understandably didn't want to get shot by trigger-happy American soldiers. So he tried to escape through the tunnel. Anyway, we had agreed to let him go because we only wanted Duri. But the General changed things at the last minute."

Buzz still needed convincing. "Something's not right."

"I agree. Obviously the raid didn't happen as planned. We ended up with Hashimi and no General. Block was furious at first, but let up when he realized Hashimi had not double-crossed him after all. He tried to escape through the tunnel, but the General switched with him at the last minute. Makes sense to me."

Buzz finished the last beer, then stood with a slight wobble. "Thanks for the toast—and the information. I'm going to find Hashimi. Think we should put him back on a tight leash just to be safe." Buzz turned toward the door and lined up his exit path carefully.

"Wait a minute," Sedal said. "You didn't tell me how you knew about my spying on you."

Buzz peered back over his shoulder. "I caught the robot in the act. Watched him steal data through the window."

"That's it?"

"That's it."

Sedal watched the drunken cowboy amble out the door, leaving the sober former chess champion to wonder how he had ended up on the losing end of that exchange.

Chapter Thirty-Two

Buzz stumbled through the grand foyer of the main palace and found Reid working at the computer station near the kitchen. His clumsy entrance went unnoticed, mainly because soldiers came through there throughout the day. Reid was focusing on the computer, watching a digital playback of the earlier conversation in the infirmary. The final gruesome moments replayed as Duri choked the life out of the broken old man. Buzz hovered over her, trying to focus on the screen, rubbing his eyes, and swaying from side to side.

"Is that Ayad?"

The sudden intrusion startled Reid, but she quickly regained her composure. Considering the cold reception Buzz had given her outside the infirmary, she was prepared to play the role of the professional. But something in the air changed her mind quickly. "You smell terrible. Are you drunk?"

Buzz smiled sleepily and leaned in with puckered lips. Reid recoiled, pushing him away. "Hey, come on, Reid. I didn't mean to act like that earlier. I just needed to release some stress. Come on, we really don't know each other that well; and, well—I needed some downtime." He shrugged stupidly.

"No, I understand." She looked him up and down. "I hear a hot shower can calm a person down."

"Funny—so we're OK?"

"We're fine. But, I don't want you holding anything back from me. I know we sort of went too fast, but I do care about you." She slowly reached for his hand and kissed it, then softened. "I'm glad you feel better. But you picked a bad time to get drunk. That's Ayad on the video, and he's dead now."

"The, uh, meeting should have never been like that," Buzz slurred.

"I'm going to have trouble following you if you don't sober up a little." She tried again, "What do you mean?"

"I just mean the MPs are too far away."

"Ah, well, that's not the only part of this I have a problem with. Ayad seemed at ease with Duri at first, but then got scared." She backed the recording a few moments and pressed Play. "Right here. See? Duri whispers something that scares the hell out of Ayad."

"Can't hear it. May have to pay Duri a visit and beat it out of him. I'm losing my patience with him."

"Block's already ahead of you on that one. Doesn't matter, though. We know that method doesn't work with that sadist. He has almost no concept of pain. Besides, Sedal should be here soon to enhance the audio. We'll isolate and amplify the whispers using his software, and hopefully we'll be able to hear the exchange."

Reid was about to continue, but noticed Buzz shaking his head. "I left the lieutenant at the bar. He was picking up where I left off. He may be a little drunk too."

"I may be drunk, and I may be little, but I am not a little drunk." Sedal swayed as he managed his way to the coffee machine in the kitchen.

Buzz burst into sputtering laughter. "I just got that. Good one, Lieutenant."

Reid, the only sober person in the room, ducked her head into her hands. Sedal met Buzz with a high five that spilled a quarter of his coffee in all directions.

"Agent Reid, don't get up. I'll be using the computer to your right, assuming I make it there." Sedal shuffled his feet and sat in front of the computer next to Reid. Soon he had windows opening and voice analysis software functioning.

"Doesn't look like the alcohol slowed you down on the computer."

"Nope, Agent Reid, it hasn't. I may have trouble walking and talking, but on the computer, I'm right at home." Sedal typed and clicked with impressive ease, eventually opening and playing the audio file featuring Duri and Ayad. He isolated the audio segment that he needed, then displayed it as a graphic representation. "This voiceprint represents all the sounds that the mike picked up during that key point in the conversation. I can do a spectrum analysis and separate the whispers from any extra noises. Then I can amplify the conversation. Should be easy since the room was cleared out. The lowest decibel ranges should be where we find the vocal tracks we're looking for."

Buzz looked to his partner for help, but she just shrugged. They had seen this software in use, but could care less about the technical play-by-play. The voiceprint on the screen suddenly split into five separate audio spectrums and Reid slowly began to understand the process.

For Buzz, comprehension came more slowly. "The conversation is in there somewhere, right?"

"That's right my inebriated friend," said Sedal. "But they're different decibel ranges. One of these tracks should have the vocals on it. I need to find that one and clean it up."

Reid already had it all figured out. "The top two are too loud, and the third one looks like a heart monitor beeping. Plus, it's probably too loud too."

Sedal quit clicking, then looked at her in amazement. "There you go. I'm impressed."

"Don't be. Remember, I'm not drunk."

A few mouse clicks eliminated the first two voiceprints. Buzz chimed in loudly. "Oh, oh, oh! Wait! I see it now!"

Reid cringed, working her ear a little with a finger. "Hey, volume control. Besides, it's not that difficult." She looked up at him, annoyed, "You're behind, so try and keep up."

Sedal removed the third track, then played an amplified clone of the fourth audio file. Certain segments of words punctuated the garbled background noise. He tried the last file and it sounded similar. "Looks like these two need to be combined. And that should do the trick."

As promised, the final product had only human voices, first Duri's, then Ayad's. Sedal shook his head because both spoke Arabic. In the intervening silence, both men turned toward the scratching sound of Reid's pen on paper. She finished and raised the page, displaying the short transcript.

Duri: Sorry old friend. But I must ensure your silence.
Ayad: Wait, you are not the General? Who are you?

Sedal grabbed a pen and hurled it at Buzz. "I thought you went looking for Hashimi."

"I did, but I kept getting lost. He's not in his cell, and his guard doesn't have a radio."

Reid realized that something was very wrong. "He was just here. Left right before Buzz stumbled in."

"I need to talk to him," Buzz said. He was sobering up very quickly. "Sedal mentioned the blood tests matched Duri's relative in the States. Hashimi first said the general we have in custody is Duri, then he isn't. Now Ayad also says it isn't him. Somebody needs to tell me what the hell is going on."

"Well, DNA doesn't lie. People do," Reid insisted.

Sedal tried to stand. "DNA only proves who he's related to. All we know is that the man in the U.S. is related to our prisoner. And Ayad realized that man is not Duri. That couldn't have been planned. Hashimi has to be the liar."

"What do you mean?" Reid asked.

Buzz, feeling slightly more lucid, made the point as slowly and clearly as he could. "We think that Hashimi has set us up all along, trying to throw us off, confusing our investigation. The raid at the bunker happened because Block and brainiac here emailed Hashimi before the invasion. He could have told Duri, and they could have planned this whole deal together."

"Not could have; probably did," added Sedal.

Reid paced back and forth while trying to absorb this new line of thought. "OK Lieutenant, get Block and fill him in. And get back on the computer and track down Hashimi. He still has the bracelet. Buzz will help if he can." She took a long hard look at Buzz, who was standing straighter, and appeared more alert. Then she turned back to Sedal. "I'm going to contact the FBI and see if they can dig up anything on Duri's so-called brother."

Buzz said, "I wouldn't worry too much about Hashimi. He's under guard. And as long as we have Rashid and his tattoos, we still have some valuable leads to follow."

"By the way, has anyone been translating his writings?" Reid asked.

"He's still under sedation, and his condition is not that good," said Sedal. "I told that damn nurse we'd quit moving him around for now. Wouldn't want to be accused of causing a prisoner's death."

"I could give a damn right now," Reid said. "The information on him could be the most critical Intel we'll ever find. I'll go finish translating myself."

"No can do, Reid. He's in Army custody, and the Red Cross is all over us right now," said Sedal. "I got a good bit off him already, though, and Colonel Holt is going over that Intel thoroughly before they act on it. If it's bogus info, we won't need the rest anyway."

Reid nodded in frustration, then slipped away to follow the next lead. She felt like the butt of one big practical joke. The prisoners had played them in grand style, but she knew the pieces had to come together; the consequences of failure would not be the least bit amusing.

Chapter Thirty-Three

A shadowy, hooded figure slinked through the side door of the infirmary. The man hid in a dark corner of the hallway while an MP exited a room ahead. The guard walked to another door on the left, looked inside, and headed to the front of the building. The intruder carefully made his way to that same room and quickly ducked inside.

The room, darkened by black garbage bags, smelled of sweat and medicine. The sleeping patient, the tattooed Rashid, did not stir as the overhead light suddenly cast a soft glow. The masked intruder found a wooden chair in the corner, then put it to good use, tilting and wedging its back under the doorknob. Any curious guards or nurses would have to use greater force to enter, giving him extra time to escape.

The intruder prepared his exit by removing a section of the opaque garbage bags and forcing the window open. He looked around, quickly assessing his options. There were several ways he could accomplish his task, but the method did not matter. The goal was to destroy all the data Rashid's body possessed. Unfortunately for Rashid, the intruder had decided to sacrifice him for the good of the mission.

The intruder worked quickly. First he pulled out a plastic bottle of lighter fluid and hastily emptied the contents onto the bed sheets. Then, after lighting a clove cigarette, he dropped the match onto the bed near Rashid's foot. The fuel-soaked cotton accelerated the flames and the fire sprang to life. The intruder immediately moved to the final phase, plunging a hunting knife deep into the helpless man's chest while puffing casually on his cigarette. Rashid's heavy sedation made the job easier. The victim's deep breaths instantly stopped, triggering the alarms on the monitoring equipment.

Moments later, the doorknob rattled, followed by pounding and screaming. The nurse had been listening from the other room and now panicked, trying to reach her dying patient. The killer sheathed the murder weapon in the glow of the flames before moving to the window. He checked outside for activity, but felt compelled to make a quicker exit when deep voices joined that of the nurse. A mighty kick cracked the wood of the rickety chair as the killer dove through the open window. A second kick splintered the makeshift doorstop, clearing the way for the guards to enter. As planned, the fully ignited fire delayed their pursuit. Dowsing the flames became the soldier's first priority, although they were ill prepared to fight fire. By the time they realized the patient could not be saved, the killer had disappeared, and the fire had obliterated the data.

* * *

Lieutenant Sedal sat within reach of three computers, clicking away as Buzz drank his third cup of coffee. The caffeine was helping him sober up, but he still felt less than a hundred percent.

Sedal seemed less affected. "Found him!"

One more swig and Buzz headed for the console. "OK, where is the little bastard?"

"Look."

Buzz leaned in to study the map and blinking beacon at the center of the screen. "Is that…"

"Yep."

"What the hell is he doing there?"

"Don't know," said Sedal. "But it looks like he's moving to the west. Don't have a clue where his guard could be."

"I'll intercept him," Buzz declared, as he grabbed a radio and checked the magazine in his gun.

"I'll send a unit out," replied Sedal.

"Get them there ahead of me and I'll meet them," Buzz said, holstering his weapon.

"I'd prefer that you just stay here. Our soldiers will bring him in."

"You don't really think I'm staying here?"

"I can't stop you, but I think you're in no shape to…" Sedal shook his head. "What's the use; just be careful out there."

Buzz jogged away, showing signs of recovery from the alcohol. The adrenaline must have helped, Sedal thought—good. Sedal radioed the command center to request a dispatch of soldiers. He had picked a busy time, but the commanders managed to spare a small unit. Soon, three soldiers mounted a Humvee and headed across the Tigris River toward the far north side of Baghdad International Airport.

Chapter Thirty-Four

Colonel Block hovered above the soldiers working the computers below him. He paced anxiously behind his section in the command center, listening to the bad news coming in over the phone. Colonel Holt spotted him from across the room and tentatively walked in his direction.

As he approached, Holt could hear Block loudly speaking to Sedal on the other end of the line. "So you're telling me that Duri is probably not really Duri; Hashimi set us up and is escaping, and the infirmary is on fire, which, by the way, has toasted our only major source of information!"

Holt froze. He knew what he had heard was intended for his benefit, and the repercussions of the news hit him hard. If Rashid's markings really did represent the locations of WMD stockpiles, then the best hope for finding the deadly weapons had gone up in flames.

Block listened to the phone for a few more moments, then slammed it down. Holt decided to wait before confronting Block; he wanted to make sure he wouldn't get caught by flying objects. "Block, you gotta learn to control that temper. You're gonna kill one of your own men one of these days."

"Wait a minute," Block shouted. "You're no better." Then Block slammed a fist on a desk in front of him. "I just can't believe I let that little shit fool me!"

"You mean Hashimi?" Holt asked. "What about the General, or whoever he is? What are you going to do about him?"

"At least I know where he is. As long as the Red Cross doesn't pay him any more visits, I'll be fine."

"Which they will. Hell, I'd worry more about one of these reporters getting hold of this. What you've done is still torture, even if he's not a general. And your career may be over just for that."

Block stood in front of Holt, menacingly cracking his giant knuckles. "It was worth it."

"So, what do we do about Hashimi?"

"You don't have to worry about him. Not your responsibility. We're monitoring the hunt from here. Problem is, I think Sedal is drunk or tired. He kept repeating himself."

"I'd take Sedal blitzed over most people any day," Holt said.

"I agree. But, it's sometimes a curse having someone that capable. I put too much on him and expect him to be on duty twenty-four hours a day. I should have some of his duties assigned to other soldiers. It would give him some breathing room, and maybe help him get a better handle on the big picture."

"I'm guilty of that too, so don't be so hard on yourself," Holt said. "I find a good soldier and dump everything on him. Or, most recently, on her. War's different these days. Need smarter people to handle the technology. Not too many good ones around, though."

Block scanned the computer screens at his table, looking for any positive sign. "Holt, please tell me you found something useful in the initial data I gave you. We haven't."

"No, I'm afraid not. Just a series of waypoints. But without the final destination, it won't do us much good. The teams have checked the waypoint locations, but they appear to be just landmarks to follow."

"How spread out?"

"Hmm, I don't think very far apart."

"Well, that information represents about fifty percent of what was in the markings," Block said. "I'll send someone over to help do an analysis on the locations and distances. We can extrapolate the other half of the data and hopefully come up with a probable search radius. A long shot, no doubt, but it's all we've got right now."

"See what happens when you settle down and think instead of pounding your fists?" Holt said.

"I am in intelligence," Block declared, locking eyes with Holt.

Holt shook his head, then turned and left the room.

* * *

The soldiers ahead of Buzz exited the paved road onto what barely passed as grazing land for a few flocks of sheep and a number of goats. The men in the armored Humvee dismounted with weapons drawn, fully alert. Buzz approached them, riding the scooter Sedal had offered as transportation around the camp. Not ideal, but what the hell. Suddenly, he was feeling extremely vulnerable because he was still a little drunk, lightly armed, and a white man on a scooter in an unsecured area of a war zone. So he sped up to join the relative security of a small squad of slightly better armed teenagers wearing U.S. military uniforms. They welcomed him by pointing their rifles and screaming as he coasted to a stop behind them. His credentials and skin color quickly put the inexperienced men at ease.

"Don't mind me. I'm just an observer on this fox hunt," Buzz said with an awkward grin.

Some just nodded, others shrugged, then the soldier in charge had the squad return to the search. The sounds of gunfire and mortar rounds continued all around them, as usual. The sounds of war seemed much louder than back at camp, adding to the tension. The soldier in charge was talking on his satellite phone while constantly checking his handheld GPS. Buzz followed and listened, wishing he could borrow the weapon slung across the soldier's back. He felt certain the squad could deal with anything that might come up, but it was hard relying on someone else. He had always been more comfortable watching out for himself, and old habits were hard to break.

The coordinates being relayed by Sedal led the men toward the sheep, now consolidated into one flock by a wary shepherd boy. He watched with trepidation as the squad drew within a hundred yards. Buzz scanned the barren landscape, struggling to find any hole big enough for the rat he was looking for to hide in. There were none, and that sinking feeling hit him once again.

Then the soldiers stopped as the flock spread apart. The shepherd boy did his best to gather the panicked sheep and goats, but soon conceded. He moved away too, leaving a single goat behind. The emaciated animal continued to munch on a dried clump of weeds, undeterred by the activity around him. The soldier in charge decided to investigate and walked over to the goat.

In that instant, Buzz spotted the familiar black plastic collar fitted tightly around the animal's neck. He immediately keyed into the symbolism of Hashimi using a goat. The gesture was an outright insult.

Chapter Thirty-Five

Agent Reid sunk in her chair while trying to focus on the computer in front of her. Once again, the situation had spun out of control, leaving no time for little things like personal hygiene and rest. But she had her "rabbit food," as Buzz called it, and that would have to sustain her.

The small room the Army had sanctioned as a CIA office and sleeping quarters, although sparse, provided her with some much-needed peace and quiet. As she poured through new data from Langley and reports from operatives in the field, she occasionally glanced at the cot in the corner. The recent memory of her encounter with Buzz was just one more open issue as she tried to survive the boredom of information overload. And the throbbing pain in her leg, at times, completely occupied her thoughts.

More than an hour had passed since the goat was found wearing Hashimi's ankle bracelet, putting Camp Slayer on full security alert. Among the many open windows on Reid's computer screen was an activity log occasionally updated by Sedal. She had been monitoring the search for Hashimi as well as the progress of Block's plan to produce a search radius for the WMDs. Since Reid's primary objective was to find those weapons stockpiles, she had put herself directly in the loop, calling Block for regular verbal status reports. Apparently, he no longer seemed to mind sharing any and all information with the CIA.

The data coming in from Langley emanated from Reid's most recent contact with the director himself. After hearing Block's idea of establishing a search radius, she

made sure to feed Langley all information gleaned from
Rashid's markings. The analysts were already hard at
work, spurred on by the challenge of beating Army
Intelligence to the solution. As Reid perused the latest
data, she realized they may be onto something.

The waypoints all followed a historical riverbed that
had fed directly into the Tigris River during the time of
ancient Babylon. The analysts believed this to have a
symbolic significance and were studying satellite
photographs of the area from the previous ten years.
Although this might take some time, Reid was beginning
to believe the answer was most certainly there to be found.

Reid felt her heart quicken at the possibility of actually
finding WMDs, and attacked the problem with new vigor.
She had many more reports to sift through, and knowing
Buzz, she had every confidence he would somehow
manage to find Hashimi. And when he did, it gave her
great satisfaction to know that Buzz would personally
repay the bastard for his betrayal.

* * *

Hours passed, and Sedal still had no leads on Hashimi.
He had the doctors and several Intel officers examine
Rashid's burnt corpse, but nothing could be salvaged from
his skin. They did, however, find an odd piece of some
scorched object buried in the ashes on the bed. One of the
mobile labs testing it was trying to determine its
composition. Sedal could feel it coming together, but the
waiting was driving him crazy.

Sedal stopped for a short break and stared into space,
emptying his mind. He came out of his daze when he

happened to notice Buzz walking past him toward the coffee. Apparently, Buzz wasn't going to fill him in, so he decided to make the first move. "No luck?" Sedal asked, a little annoyed.

Buzz guzzled cold coffee, then flicked the rest of the foul brew into the sink. "He's long gone," Buzz said, disgusted. "Probably his plan all along. Stay close, gain our confidence, make sure all the loose ends were taken care of, then get the hell out if he could."

"If it's any consolation, Block found a way to estimate a search area for the missing weapons," Sedal offered. "That's our real target anyway, so forget about Hashimi. He'll turn up somewhere. For now, Reid needs your help sorting through data and reviewing reports. Langley took Block's idea and is probably going to pinpoint the stockpiles."

"I'll go help her then," Buzz muttered. "You're right about Hashimi, though. His work is done. We should focus on Duri now. Anything else on him?"

Sedal held up a finger while wheeling his chair to a different computer. "Now that you mention it, that's been my primary objective for the past few hours."

Buzz circled around the equipment and stood beside Sedal. "You didn't find him, did you?" Buzz asked.

"No, but I did confirm, by using facial recognition software, that the man we have is not Duri. At least that's the best determination I could make using these photos." Sedal pulled up side-by-side photos on the screen. "The picture on the left is the real Duri taken from a DOD database. The one on the right deserves an Oscar for his performance. He's not Duri, though, just a very good imposter. And he's a pretty damn good killer too, but we're not sure of his real identity."

"So if he just disappeared, then no one would notice."

"He's already registered as a POW, so they know we have someone they think is Duri. It's been reported in the news," Sedal pointed out.

"Damn! So how'd the blood samples match?" Buzz asked.

"Thought you'd never ask. The FBI did some checking with Immigration, and that guy they caught entered the U.S. using some very good false documentation. He's related to the guy we have, but not to the real Duri. It confirms my photo analysis."

"So we have no leads on the real Duri?" Buzz asked.

"Ah, wait. That's not all. Langley informed Reid that a picture from a Saudi airport camera shows the General boarding a plane headed for Pakistan. He used a previously unknown alias and, again, very good false documents."

"Shit," Buzz said, then stamped his foot in frustration.

Sedal pulled up another picture to compare with the DOD file version. Buzz sensed something wrong immediately. "Problem. Why'd he look right at the camera? The General would be smarter than that."

"You must be sober now," Sedal said. "It's not Duri. Just another imposter. Not nearly as good as ours, but they knew he'd pass as Duri on the grainy airport cameras."

"That son-of-a-bitch has got more doubles than Saddam," Buzz hissed. So where's the real one?"

"Don't know," admitted Sedal. "But it probably matters as much as finding Hashimi."

"And what if Rashid was just another decoy?"

Sedal thought a moment, hesitating to consider the possibility. "But they went through the trouble of burning his body," Sedal complained, a little uncertain now.

"Can't rule anything out, Lieutenant. Hashimi's job was to keep us off the trail of the person holding the real information. This is probably just another delaying tactic. They've layered this plan with so many decoys and imposters, we may never figure out who's who." Buzz couldn't help a sour grin of admiration for the deceptive bastards.

"Damn, you're right. But why didn't they just give up this information before the war? Would've been much easier. Perhaps we wouldn't have gone through with the invasion," Sedal said.

"They couldn't be sure of that," replied Buzz. "The way we monitored every email, phone call, radio contact, and every movement they made leading up to the invasion. Besides, this was a last ditch move. And if we didn't really attack, they figured they'd keep the information to themselves. As a matter of fact, I think they were convinced we were just bluffing anyway. But Duri concocted this plan assuming we would invade. He knew they couldn't stop the coalition in a ground war, and all would be lost. So here we have Saddam's final revenge. Give the terrorists the weapons, and let them raise hell. And the WMDs were probably being moved around right up until the invasion. That's why they waited."

"But why wouldn't they use the weapons themselves?" Sedal asked.

"That would only slow our attack and kill our soldiers, not to mention put Saddam himself at risk. He didn't want to be caught upwind. This is a better revenge for the

Iraqis. They know terrorists will use the weapons on Americans—on American soil."

"Makes sense," Sedal conceded. "You've thought a lot about this, huh?"

"The CIA has—as a matter of planning. I'm surprised you haven't considered these possibilities."

"Give me a break, will you. I've been in Afghanistan for two years, rooting out Taliban and al Qaeda one by one. Haven't had time to look at the big picture in Iraq."

"Well, I'm gonna sum it up for you the way I see it," Buzz said. General Duri is out there, and so is Hashimi. I want them both. One of them has that information, and they're planning on giving it away to terrorists."

Sedal nodded his agreement as Buzz walked away. "Maybe he's already given it to them," Sedal called out as Buzz reached the door.

Buzz stopped, struck by the fact that this had not occurred to anyone at the CIA or Army Intelligence until that moment. The thought that they may already be too late turned Buzz's stomach. He pounded a fist on the doorframe as he left the room, taking this dire possibility as motivation to work faster.

Chapter Thirty-Six

Hashimi navigated a small wooden fishing boat along the Iraqi bank of the Shatt al Arab River, a few kilometers southeast of Basrah. The trolling motor at the front of the vessel had steadily pulled him away from the port city for the previous two hours. Now the engine started to stall. Hashimi shook the empty gasoline container and cursed the setting sun. He searched the riverbank frantically, looking for a sign meant for his eyes. But he worried that finding a white flag hanging on the back of a building would be impossible in this low light.

The boat inched closer to shore, causing the propeller blades to flirt with the shallow muddy flats. Then the motor quit. Hashimi huffed furiously as he tilted the propeller out of the water and grabbed the oar. Now he would have to paddle or walk, and he knew his contact would not be looking for him on land.

Luckily, Hashimi only had to labor for a few minutes. From a built-up area on the bank ahead, a flashlight blinked in code. The contact had probably spotted him using night vision binoculars. Always good to have a plan B, thought Hashimi, as he increased his speed.

Soon, he closed in on a short fishing pier and tied his boat off, though he did not need to bother. The 22-foot Sea Ray that occupied the opposite side of the pier would be his early morning escape craft. Hashimi smiled to himself. After enduring the creeping trolling motor, and even slower rowing, he was looking forward to the extra horsepower of the larger boat on the open sea.

Hashimi slowly climbed a short set of steps that led the weary traveler to the top of a stone wall, and then onto the grounds of a large concrete building. Armed men roamed the property, smoking and looking in all directions. None of them gave him a second look, except for one very imposing man leaning against the compound wall, and diligently tugging at his mustache.

Hashimi drew a deep breath, then approached his general. He grew more nervous and excited with each step. They embraced and greeted each other in the traditional manner. Duri managed a warm smile before debriefing his subordinate. "Is everything taken care of?"

"Yes, General. They know that Majid is your imposter, but that is not a problem."

"He is still alive?"

"Yes, but all others are dead. He has been beaten and injured by the Americans."

For a moment, Duri's expression changed. "The Americans. They are hypocrites. They speak of treating people humanely, and yet they are no better than anyone else." Just as suddenly, his good mood returned as he pulled out a pack of cigarettes. "You have nothing to smoke my friend? How long has it been?"

Hashimi could barely contain his excitement. The General knew him well, handing him a clove cigarette and a lighter. "You forget, General. I can be very persuasive. They were ready to give me a house in Connecticut."

Duri actually laughed. Surprising behavior for a man not known for his sense of humor, Hashimi thought.

"You are a very interesting and resourceful man," Duri said. "But this is why you were chosen for the mission."

Hashimi lit his cigarette and enjoyed a long pull. "The Americans still think the weapons are in Iraq."

This brought more laughter. "Where do they think they are hidden?"

"The last I heard, they only have the information off of part of Rashid's body. I burned him before they finished reading the tattoos," Hashimi said. "I even turned off the water to the building so he would burn completely."

"I wonder if the CIA has found the old river bed?" Duri mused.

"They probably have. I wish I could watch them as they try to search the desert for buried weapons."

"And what about the device?" Duri asked.

"It was destroyed in the fire."

Duri started walking slowly toward a door, then motioned for Hashimi to follow. "Did you see any British patrols near us?"

"They are all over the port, in the water and on land," Hashimi said. "The focus is on controlling Basrah. They will spread out soon to secure the river."

"Then we will be fine," said the General. "Get some rest. You leave in a few hours."

"A few hours? I thought we were to leave in the morning?"

"There has been one last change of plans. A final diversion."

Hashimi crushed out his cigarette, then saluted the General before stepping into the building. Duri stayed outside to watch the sun sink below the horizon. Then somewhere in the enveloping darkness, he heard a low hum. He turned his head, trying to pinpoint a direction, but quickly realized the noise came from above, fading quickly. By the time he searched the night sky using his night vision binoculars, the machine had moved on. Duri would not sleep that night.

* * *

Buzz approached CIA headquarters and peered through the small window in the door. He could see Reid from the back, apparently hard at work on the computer. When Buzz entered the room, she did not stir, so he stepped silently behind her and placed his hands gently on her shoulders. Apparently, she had fallen asleep over her terminal, exhausted from reviewing countless files.

Reid jerked around, nearly standing before relaxing in relief. Buzz held a finger to his mouth and sat her back down. Neither spoke as he massaged the tension away from her shoulders. His injured shoulder burned a little, but that didn't matter. He enjoyed the feeling of her giving in to his touch, her tight muscles melting at his fingertips. She needed this. And so did he.

After a few minutes she reached back and pulled both of his arms down across her chest until his face met hers. They kissed, slowly at first, then more passionately. Buzz could feel her firm body push into his, aching for him. Buzz finally broke it off. He leaned against the desk, catching his breath. Reid was looking at him, her face red, still a little hot. He exhaled, then noticed her knowing smile. He had almost lost himself again, but snapped back to reality.

"Reid, we can't do this now. Too much work to do."

"There's always too much work," she said.

Then she kissed him again, hoping to break his will. He pulled away, trying to catch his breath. She playfully acted hurt at the rejection, and frowned.

"You're sexy when you do that," Buzz admitted. He straightened up and stepped away. "So stop it—OK?"

Reid laughed, then looking back at the screen, she slowly exhaled. "Fine—you're right. We have work to do."

"Good," Buzz said, a little uncertain. "Now go for a walk, stretch your muscles, get some air. I'll get started in here."

Reid stood. "I like that suggestion. OK, but I'll be back with some food. I'll get you something nice and greasy." She smiled coyly, then winked.

"You know me a little too well," Buzz said.

As Reid turned and headed for the door, Buzz stopped her. "What do I need to be doing?"

"Oh, just keep in touch with Langley, watch Sedal's activity logs, call Block for an update, track any unusual transmissions, and find Hashimi and Duri—that's all."

"OK, should have that wrapped up by dinner time," Buzz gibed.

Reid blew him a kiss and left him to get started. He was hoping to catch a break, but knew luck was their only hope now.

Chapter Thirty-Seven

Colonel Block lumbered through the quiet palace halls just after four o'clock in the morning. Sedal followed until they reached the CIA office. Block grabbed the knob, but Sedal hedged.

"Colonel, considering the agents' unique working relationship, we should probably knock first."

"Oh hell, Lieutenant. How else are we gonna have any fun?"

"That's true. But you first, just in case they start shooting," Sedal cautioned.

Without hesitation, Block barged into the room. The scene inside was disappointing. Buzz knocked over a can of soda on his desk, trying to get to his gun, and Reid fell from her cot. Block had been hoping for something a little more compromising, but they had both been sleeping.

Buzz rubbed his bleary eyes, then threw a stale, half-eaten fried pie at the intruders. "Sorry to disappoint you gentlemen, but, as you can see, we've been working all night."

Reid grabbed her sore leg and began rubbing it, but stayed on the floor. "We didn't get anywhere last night. Hope you boys did better."

Block never missed an opportunity to do you one better. He glanced over at Sedal and nodded. Sedal stepped forward and handed both agents aerial photographs.

Buzz got to his feet. "Looks like a compound manned by militia. What's this got to do with us?"

Sedal encouraged him to look closer. "See the boat?"

"I see it. A lot nicer than the crappy little fishin' boats I've seen all over this place."

"Yep, nice little operation going on there," Sedal said. "It's southeast of Basrah on the Shatt al Arab River. The Brits have been focusing on securing the city and the port. Haven't had a chance to lock down these other pockets of resistance."

Reid leaned back against the bed, stretching her arms while Sedal watched. "That's going to be a problem for a long time, for us, and for the Brits. Like chasing fire ant mounds around the back yard."

"Nice analogy, Reid," Buzz said admiringly, momentarily longing for a visit home. "You sure you've never been to Texas?" She answered with a flirtatious wink. He paused, then reluctantly turned his attention back to business. "So Lieutenant, what does this have to do with our mission?"

Sedal straightened the glasses on his sharp beaky nose, which reminded Buzz of a strict schoolteacher he'd once had, then managed to look away from Reid. He produced another set of pictures that really got their attention. "These were taken a couple of hours after the aerials. Command processed the pictures at about midnight and ordered a British recon team in to check it out. We just finished confirming that this is the real Duri a few minutes ago. Matched up pretty well using facial recognition."

Buzz studied the face for a few seconds before gearing up. "What about Hashimi?"

"Nothing on him so far. Could be in the compound. Maybe he's nowhere close to Duri."

Block, who had been content to let his lieutenant explain, decided to interject. "Sedal's going with you."

Buzz paused and checked for confirmation. Sedal acted like an eight-year-old about to go on recess. "We're getting a chopper ready right now. The PackBot's being loaded, but we can leave as soon as we get there."

The thought of another colleague being lost in the field briefly crossed Buzz's mind, but he quickly put the notion down. Instead of objecting, as his instincts told him, Buzz gave Sedal a nod. "Well then, I guess that makes you my new partner."

"I guess it does," Sedal said.

"Good. Let's go," Buzz replied, then helped Reid off the floor and back onto her cot.

When he looked back to the colonel, Buzz could see that Block was finding it hard to send his best soldier into the line of fire.

As he stepped through the doorway, Block clinched his teeth. "Doug, be careful."

"Yes, Colonel, I will," Sedal said.

After Block left, Buzz grabbed his pack and motioned to Sedal that they were leaving. But the lieutenant had turned away, and was staring at the door. "What's wrong?" Buzz asked.

"Sorry, it's just that he's never called me by my first name before," Sedal said.

"Damn, you act like he's your daddy."

Sedal gave Buzz a look like he had hit a nerve. "Let's go."

"Sorry."

The two men started for the door, but Reid caught Buzz by the arm. "Wait, aren't you going to say goodbye?" she whispered.

Buzz looked at Sedal, slightly embarrassed. Reid was just sitting there, looking seductive. "Yeah," Buzz said.

As Buzz bent down toward Reid, she got up and limped right past him. When she reached Sedal, she gave him a short kiss on the lips. "Bye, Doug."

Buzz watched Sedal turn red, then stare at him, wide-eyed. Buzz couldn't help cracking a wide grin.

"OK, I'm ready now, Buzz" said Sedal. But he knew not to press his luck. "I'll meet you at the foyer." He smiled and left.

Buzz waved him off without looking, then pulled Reid into his chest. "Highly inappropriate."

"You'll have to punish me when you get back," she teased.

"If I don't make it, I give you permission to date Block."

"What about Doug?"

"He's off limits."

For a long moment, they gazed at each other, wanting to stay in the embrace. "Now look here cowboy," Reid said finally. "You've been enough of a hero for a lifetime. Be careful—OK?"

"I could never make up for what happened to Naseth. I owe him the best I got every chance I get. And you know better than anyone how important it is to find these men. I'd give my life to stop them."

She nodded, then looked at the floor. He could see the pain in her eyes; she knew he was right. He kissed her goodbye, then held her again before turning away and leaving.

Reid watched him step through the door. He didn't look back.

Chapter Thirty-Eight

The transport helicopter carrying Buzz and Sedal approached the encircled compound at low altitude, landing behind a group of buildings and armored vehicles. As soon as it touched down, they piled out ahead of the other soldiers, both eager to catch the men responsible for their recent sleep deprivation. They headed straight for the forward British units, who were already taking small arms fire from the compound windows and rooftop. The sun rose fast across the water, directly behind a building casting a broad shadow. They knew that the impending light would soon blind them at that angle.

Buzz reached an armored vehicle manned by four British soldiers who were busy ducking bullets. Sedal followed closely and the two men started immediately assessing the situation. After a quick look around, Buzz saw an obvious problem.

"Damn! We can't even get a good look! Too dangerous to stick our heads up!"

Sedal smiled and opened his pack, then pulled out the PackBot's remote control and a radio. "I'll make sure the robot's unloaded! Where do you want me to send it?"

Buzz moved to the right side of the vehicle and surveyed the other units set up near the water. "Those soldiers are keeping their heads up. Looks like they're a little farther away from the building. And they seem to have a good angle."

The soldier nearest Buzz peeked around the corner and started nodding. "Sir, that's an affirmative! There are no windows on that side of the building."

"Good," Buzz barked. "We need to get to that position. Flank the PackBot around that side and we'll follow."

The soldier offered another bit of useful information. "Sir, we've been holding back waiting on you. Just say the word and we'll give some cover fire."

"That'll do just fine," Buzz said. "Wait for my signal and tell your boys to pepper the concrete around the windows for now, if they can. We don't want anyone dead in there until we know who's inside."

The soldier relayed the instructions to the squad commanders using his radio. Sedal was already sending the PackBot in a wide loop to the compound's right flank. Buzz watched the screen on the remote until the Brits came into view. "OK, Lieutenant. Get it behind that pile of junk next to the building."

"Looks like some of their transportation. Got a few motorcycles in there. That's pretty close to the building, though. Sure you want it there?"

"Yes, but scan the area first," Buzz ordered. "Check the rooftop too."

The gunfire died out and the air grew quieter, giving Sedal the opportunity to investigate the surroundings more thoroughly. He panned the PackBot's camera to the roof, then zoomed in on the three gunmen peeking over the ledge. "You've got to let me take those guys out," Sedal said.

"Why?" Buzz asked.

"I haven't shot any bad guys in a while, and none of them look important."

Buzz looked at him, a little unsure. "What are you gonna shoot 'em with?"

203

Sedal panned the camera down and to the right, finding the British vehicles with ten soldiers squatting behind them. "See that sniper rifle on his back?" Sedal asked.

"I'll let you shoot just one. Don't need to be wasting too much time."

"Fair enough." Sedal turned the PackBot back toward the motorcycles and accelerated the machine. The men on the roof fired a few rounds and Buzz decided to order cover fire. With a wave of his hand, the entire surrounding force let loose. As soon as the PackBot made it safely to cover, Sedal and Buzz ran for the right flank.

They jumped in behind the firing soldiers and the shooting stopped in a wave from right to left. Buzz caught his breath and stretched his wounded shoulder. "I'm beginning to think we ought to just kill 'em all, Lieutenant."

"We can't do that. Don't want to destroy any data they might be carrying."

"I know, I know," Buzz said. "I'm just tired and sore."

Sedal turned to the squad and searched for one soldier in particular. "I need the sniper rifle," he said.

The young man carrying the weapon stepped forward and handed it to him. "Yes sir, Lieutenant. Get one for me too, will you?"

Sedal nodded, then set up at the hood of one of the vehicles. The rooftop gunmen were just starting to get brave again, poking their heads up and moving around, following the heavy barrage.

Buzz tapped Sedal on the shoulder. "Ten bucks says you don't get one on the first shot."

Just on cue, the first head to pop up appeared directly in the crosshairs. "You got a bet," Sedal grinned. He steadied his aim and fired. The gunman jerked violently backward.

"A perfect shot," Buzz said admiringly.

Sedal picked up the remote control in one hand and extended the other. Buzz handed him the money. "Easy money, huh, Lieutenant?" Then, grudgingly, Buzz added, "I have to admit, you're a good shot."

Sedal pocketed the bills and exchanged the gun for the remote. He quickly maneuvered the robot to the back corner of the building without incident. Then he carefully extended the camera arm past the corner and found no activity at the back of the building. A quick scan of the pier showed the high-powered boat still waiting.

The PackBot rounded the corner and slowly crept along the wall. Buzz grew wary. "We don't have any watercraft in the area, do we?"

"Afraid not," Sedal confirmed. But they sent a Predator to watch the river. Should be here soon. Remember, this all just came together and the Brits are stretched pretty thin right now."

"That's why we're here," Buzz said.

Silence followed as the PackBot neared a closed metal door. Sedal guided the machine away from the wall and aimed it directly at the door from a few feet away. Just as the robot started forward, the door swung wide. Sedal froze and the PackBot stopped. Then a familiar face emerged from the darkness inside.

Duri stepped into the light and raised an RPG launcher directly aimed at the camera. Buzz sighed helplessly. "Get it out of there."

Sedal tried. He whipped the PackBot to the left and gave it full power. The violent shaking of the camera made it difficult to guide, though he kept it fairly straight. But the PackBot did not get far. The explosion could be heard in the distance, just as the screen turned to static.

Sedal dropped the remote to the ground and followed Buzz to the right of the squad. From there, they could see the boat and steps leading down to the pier. Buzz stepped out to get a look at the back door, but shots from the roof changed his mind. The squad commander, who had been mostly quiet, ran up to him. "You want us to keep 'em quiet?"

"Hell, yes!" Buzz snapped.

The commander turned to his squad and gave the signal. All hell broke loose, and Buzz ran back into the open. He returned shortly with bad news.

"Lieutenant! Duri's outside and men are streaming out!"

The squad commander heard this too and called for backup. Armored cars full of men immediately moved toward them. Sedal grabbed the rifle and darted into the open with Buzz close behind. He fixed Duri in the scope, then scanned the other men. It didn't take long for Hashimi to appear and follow Duri to the pier. Buzz could see them separate from the pack in a full run. "Is that Duri?"

"Yes, and Hashimi too!" Sedal yelled.

"Try to put a bullet in the boat's motor! I'm going to get some transportation!" Buzz called out.

The cover fire allowed Buzz to reach the motorcycles safely and he tried to start one with no luck. But the second one he jumped on, an ancient machine, sputtered to life. After a quick warm-up, Buzz raced over to the squad commander. Above the yelling, gunfire, and the roaring of the engine, he asked for another favor.

"Do whatever you want to that building. Just don't touch those two guys running for the boat," Buzz said.

"Right!" The commander turned to his squad and they snaked toward the compound. Soon the Brits joined in and hit the compound from all sides. The gunmen guarding the back door took the brunt of the firepower.

Buzz saluted Sedal while speeding past him, then jumped the bike over the side of a stone wall above the river, ignoring the pain in his shoulder. He landed hard on the flats of the riverbank below, but recovered nicely. The pier stood nearly three hundred yards away, and Buzz accelerated toward it. Duri and Hashimi were jumping into the boat, and he feared they might get away. With his foot, Buzz slammed the bike into high gear and pushed it as hard as it could go.

As he closed in, Buzz could see Duri pushing the boat away from the wooden pier. Then Hashimi, who was already in the driver's seat, happened to look in his direction from behind the wheel. After some pointing and shouting, Duri was made to realize Buzz was coming. Buzz kept the throttle wide open while pulling his sidearm, wishing he had more power. He was now within fifty yards of the pier, but the boat had already begun to turn away from land.

Buzz raised his gun as Duri shouldered his favorite weapon, an RPG launcher. Buzz fired, but Duri had already sent a grenade his way. The General led his shot well. The ground in front of the speeding motorcycle exploded, and the front wheel dipped violently into the resulting crater. Buzz flew over the handlebars and landed hard on his back on the gravelly soil.

The boat sped away from the bank, taking fire from Sedal's rifle. But the small boat was moving too fast and was too far away for an effective shot. Duri and Hashimi were getting away, heading for the Persian Gulf, and all Sedal could do was stand and watch.

Sedal lowered the rifle and called headquarters on his satellite phone. "Colonel. The boat carrying Duri and Hashimi is heading for open water." Sedal listened to the response, then looked to the sky. "Yes, Colonel, I see it."

The Predator had arrived, armed with a single hellfire missile. Sedal set the phone down and acquired the speeding target in the rifle's scope. He had been waiting for a moment like this and would enjoy witnessing the grand finale for himself.

For a split second, something flashed, and an instant later, a ball of fire engulfed the boat. Sedal watched as burning shreds of material fell in a large perimeter around where the boat had been seconds before. He slowly raised the phone. "Colonel, I wish you could have seen this in full color."

Then Sedal disconnected the call without signing off. He needed to get to Buzz as quickly as possible. He found a medic and a vehicle to shuttle him to the steps. As they rushed to the pier, Buzz stood, dusting himself off. He bled from many parts of his body and probably had broken bones, but there he stood, laughing out loud.

Buzz turned away from the water and saw Sedal out of the corner of his eye. He raised his arms to the sky and screamed like a lunatic. "Lieutenant! Did you see that? Bastards didn't stand a chance!"

Sedal stopped while the medic rushed ahead. "Yeah, I saw it! We had 'em right where we wanted 'em!"

The catharsis helped Buzz ignore the pain, temporarily at least. But, in truth, he knew the crash had done a good deal of damage. He tried to take a step, and collapsed into the arms of the medic.

Chapter Thirty-Nine

Reid stepped into the infirmary and sniffed. A burnt smell still lingered in the air. Buzz lay unconscious in the same area where Duri's imposter had murdered the old man. She thought this might be a bad omen, and considered having him moved.

The doctor saw Reid coming and grabbed his clipboard. "He's got an extensive list of injuries," the doctor explained. He looked up, then followed Reid's eyes to Buzz, whose shallow breathing seemed labored. "Broken ribs, assorted broken bones, and a concussion. But considering the spill he took, it could have been much worse."

Reid thanked the doctor and he left them alone. She held his good hand and hoped he would wake up, if only for a moment. Then she kissed him lightly on the cheek, and saw that her wish had been granted.

Buzz opened his eyes and took a moment to gather his senses. "What the hell is burning?"

"Try not to move too much," Reid said. "You'll regret it if you do."

Buzz gave a slight nod. Everything on his body hurt anyway, no sense in making it worse. "What about the weapons? You found any yet?" he rasped.

"We have a search radius, and I've sent the mobile labs out. But my gut tells me we won't find anything. And some of the Intel coming in from other prisoners doesn't give us much hope either," Reid admitted.

"Well at least we kept terrorists from knowing where to look," Buzz said.

"Looks like it." Reid's voice held a touch of skepticism, but Buzz didn't notice. She reached into her pocket and pulled out a plastic bag. "This is the strange object we pulled out of Rashid's ashes. It's a memory stick. Like the ones we're using in our USB ports," Reid explained.

"What was it doing there?"

"Good question. Maybe he had it in his pocket and we missed it somehow. It was found near his hip."

"Doesn't make sense," Buzz whispered. "I'm sure his pockets were checked."

"You shouldn't worry about it now. You'll just get a headache."

"No kidding." Buzz tried to smile. "I'm pretty spaced out anyway."

"That's the concussion," Reid said.

Buzz tried to rub his temples to relax the pain away. Reid took over, and he closed his eyes, enjoying her gentle touch. "I wish I could have gotten there quicker," Buzz said.

"You did fine, cowboy. Nothing you could do. The important thing is we stopped that information from falling into the wrong hands. You did your job."

Reid saw that he had fallen back to sleep, and stopped massaging his head. She had work to do now, and she knew that Buzz would recover in time. Sleep would do him more good than any treatment. With a final kiss to his forehead, Reid slipped quietly away.

* * *

Several weeks after watching General Duri perish on the Shatt al Arab River, Hashimi climbed a steep slope somewhere in the mountains of eastern Afghanistan. The loose dirt and rocks slipped from under his feet, but he slowly ascended until he reached a narrow pass flanked by rock ledges. The trail narrowed and finally flattened.

Hashimi rested on a boulder, catching his breath in the high altitude. Soon a group of five gunmen emerged on horseback further up the pass, their images silhouetted against the setting sun. Hashimi took a deep breath and walked to their position. The group leader dismounted and welcomed him with open arms. After they exchanged greetings, Hashimi removed his coat and shirt. Then, he unsheathed the hunting knife he had taken from his guard at the American base in Iraq.

The leader examined the stitches on the beleaguered traveler's abdomen and nodded. The incision had been explained to Colonel Block as a recent emergency appendectomy, one of many deceptions. Hashimi pressed the knife blade against his own skin and placed the leather sheath between his teeth. He bit down hard as the blade cut along the fresh scar line. The knife fell to the ground and Hashimi reached into the shallow cut, withdrawing a small, sealed plastic bag covered in blood.

Two of the gunmen dismounted and rushed to Hashimi's aid, immediately stitching the wound. The leader took the bag and cut into the package with the bloody knife. Inside, he found a memory stick in perfect condition.

As the sun descended on the arid land, the gunmen mounted their horses with the weakened Hashimi in tow.